Clarence B. Collins

Tom and Joe

Two farmer boys in war and peace and love. A Louisiana memory.

Clarence B. Collins

Tom and Joe
Two farmer boys in war and peace and love. A Louisiana memory.

ISBN/EAN: 9783337224165

Printed in Europe, USA, Canada, Australia, Japan

Cover: Foto ©Andreas Hilbeck / pixelio.de

More available books at **www.hansebooks.com**

TWO FARMER BOYS IN WAR AND
PEACE AND LOVE.

A LOUISIANA MEMORY.

RICHMOND, VA.:
EVERETT WADDEY, PUBLISHER AND PRINTER,
1890.

PREFACE.

⸺

THE following little story, as told by one who witnessed many of its scenes and incidents, will appeal to the hearts of thousands who saw the great drama of a quarter of a century ago. To the middle-aged and the old of our dear Southland it will bring back that happy period when our country lived its golden age--the glorious summer day that closed in storm and darkness ; to the young it tells how their ancestors lived and loved and died ; to those who loved and still love the "Lost Cause," it will recall the tenderest memories of a lifetime, and to those who loved it not, the story tells how we loved it. The love Judge Mabry bore for the Union had its counterpart all over the South, and it lasted to his dying day, but he loved better the autonomy of States. With him local pride was above and beyond national greatness. His sons were representative boys of the heroic age of our country, of such stuff as made that great struggle immortal, and made possible a glorious "New South." They were farmer boys, proud of their occupation, and glorying in their identity with the class who ruled America during seventy progressive years. Many of the incidents are literally true, and all are founded upon facts in the lives of our two boys. This story is told that our young people of to-day may not be ignorant of the more glorious "Old South."

INDEX.

TOM AND JOE.

CHAPTER I.

A GREAT EVENT.

UPON one of the lofty hills in the western suburb of Mississippi's capital city stood, many years ago, a square brick residence of comfortable proportions and design, but without any especial architectural attractiveness. It was a genuine, old-fashioned Southern home, surrounded by a charming grove of natural forest, where the broad-leafed hickory and mighty oak tempered the summer heat and flamed out in gold and scarlet when the frosts and winds of autumn came to ripen the nuts or carpet the earth with leaves. In rear and away down the sunny slope towards the river stretched garden and orchard famous for the good things so delightful to our human tastes, while in one corner of the grove nestled a little lake, where happy children sailed their toy boats on pleasant afternoons and filled the air with music of their glad young voices.

Here lived a man much loved and honored by the people; a man whose public career was as unblemished as his private character, which was severe in its purity.

In such a home Tom awoke one morning and began with clenched fists to fight the battle of life. The good man who lived there was Tom's father, and from the fact that Tom was the fifth step in the juvenile stairway, we are not justified in believing that there was any great overflow of parental joy on that occasion, but rather a sigh of relief that he was not "twins," or even a girl.

Some persons object to girls in the family, with the plea that they are more expensive and not so useful as boys. For the same coarse reason they banish roses and lilies from the garden. Our hero's after-life failed to develop the slightest cause for classing him among such persons; on the contrary, he early developed a fondness for the other sex that did more honor to his heart than to his judgment, and laid the foundation for many a future heartache. Doubtless he began by loving his mother, but that sweet woman faded away soon after his birth, leaving only a tender memory for his love, and he was bereft of that influence to which so many of the great ones of earth attribute their success.

We have stated that Tom was number five. There were three girls, and then there was Joe. Ah! yes, there was Joe. When Tom awoke he found Joe there waiting for him; had been waiting nearly five years, so now he was satisfied, and in great glee he raced out to the stable to tell old Don Pedro, the family horse, and to the kennel behind the chicken-house, where Blucher, the veteran watch-dog, had of late years done most of his watching. Both those faithful animals testified their joy at the news in a manner peculiar to such creatures, and fell to fighting the fly or the flea with renewed activity.

The local newspaper recorded the arrival of a new boy at Judge Mabry's in the usual witty style of such announcements, never thinking that it was toying with the most sacred and solemn event of family life. Relatives, both distant and at a distance, were duly notified, but the innocent hope that silver-spoons, hobby-horses, cradles, or other customary gifts would follow this notification was never realized, and there comes down to us a dim tradition that the baby was rocked in the rounding top of an ancient hair-trunk. If there were any other demonstrations at the time history fails to record them, and only the solemn fact remains that a boy, a baby boy, an embryo man, full of life and prepared for a large average of fun and tears, had come with a fixed purpose to remain as long as possible, and get the most good out of life.

During the first four years of life our little Tom did nothing remarkable. He had measles and whooping-cough just as other boys, and he fell into the river one day to be fished out more than half dead. He early displayed an alarming propensity to play out in the street and get run over by passing carriages. With that fatality attached to chubby juveniles he always

stubbed his toe at the wrong time, and never ran from
danger without falling in its pathway.   In their wanderings about the streets of the city his companions
often found stray dimes, or pocket-knives, but Tom
never did.   Joe was a lucky boy.   He always fell on his
feet, and was a leader among the West End boys, coupling a conscientious care with absolute fearlessness.

It was rare sport for the boys in those good old days
at Jackson to guy the drivers and throw clods of dirt
at the two-horse stages, but when one thundered by in
all the glory of four steeds, and the *tra-la-la-la* of the
bugles, they all stood in open-mouthed awe and each
one mentally vowed that one day he would drive a
four-horse stage.   Few boys of thirty years ago but
were guilty of such ambition which eventually they
were glad to "fling away," and admire the dashing
brakesman with brass buttons, braided cap, and impudent manner, as he tenderly assists the pretty girls off
the train and allows the old lady with a dozen bundles
to fall off if she likes.

Tom doubtless lived very happily during those four
years.   He fared well, grew amazingly, and in common
with most boys of his day and age was not too much ham-
pered by the conventionalities of dress.   In fact, a single loose garment, none too long, gave free play to the
bounding activity of the boy, and causes him after
thirty long years to sigh for his old-time freedom.

It is a pity that children are so much dressed now-
a-days.   Many of them never know the freedom and
unfettered joys of childhood; they are little old men

and women when they ought to be throwing mud at a two-horse stage. We find the little things crowding the places of amusement, balls, matinees and card parties without end, until we wonder what will be the effect upon the next generation. Do we forget that those children are to be the fathers and mothers of our race?

Tom ought to be glad that he lived in the days of stage coaches and single garments.

Well, the four years passed and our little man was four years wiser. He had learned many things that children ought to know, and the reverse; he had spent two seasons over the river at the farm and knew how to chase rabbits, find hen nests and dig worms for bait. He could do anything that a four-year-old was able to do, and he had learned that in all well-regulated families there was kept "a rod in pickle" for unruly boys. He was the strong impersonation of youth and health, with a blending of town and country manners. Joe was his tutor and leader in all things as he was his champion in many a "rough-and-tumble" of later boyhood. He forced upon the younger brother a portion of his own self-reliant courage and made good impressions upon the boy that no time nor trouble could efface. There is no teacher for imitative and confiding youth like an elder brother, and happy is the boy or girl whose big brother is a worthy and affectionate model.

Four happy and progressive years for Tom, following Joe about the streets of the city and along the banks of beautiful Pearl river, then came a great change.

CHAPTER II.

THE FIRST RIVER JOURNEY.

FOR many an age the crowning theme of poet's verse and orator's most glowing period has been woman. From empress to peasant her praises have been sung. As lover, wife, mother, and widow, her virtues are upon every manly tongue. Men do battle in her behalf. They lie, steal, and kill on her account, and they perform deeds of heroism or sacrifice in her presence that make them famous through all coming years. In every stage of life there is some one to laud her, but when she takes up the burdens of another who has fallen in the struggle, and as mother to children whose baby hands never pressed her bosom until the thrill of holy motherhood quivered through all her soul and body, then her ear listens vainly for words of commendation. Heroic, self-sacrificing stepmother! When Tom reached his fifth year his father married again, and brought into his family a woman who was henceforward to carry all the vexatious burdens incident to the life of a stepmother, but she was a noble woman and did her duty. The children all learned to love her, and as they never purposely vex those whom they love, her life was a happy one. Tom, owing to his extreme youth, was her favorite, yet she did not spoil him on that account. She was a stepmother in name but a mother in fact, and she soon taught him that there was a mysterious place known as the "far room," to which he was often invited. The irrepressible spirit of mischief in the boy had to be warred against, when in mere wantonness he twisted the tails of the calves to hear them bleat, tied the cat with a twine to old Blucher, or cast his father's boots into the well; and the sounds of wailing and woe that came up from that distant room told of penance and well-grounded regrets.

It may be that we punish too much. We cannot, in our maturer years and feelings, countenance many of the pranks in which our boyhood gloried. We are elder tyrants, constantly warring against the exuberance of childhood. Grown-up people forget sometimes that a healthy boy must have fun, if every quadruped and biped on the farm has to suffer.

When the father married he not only obtained a good wife, but sundry servants, plantations, live-stock, etc., all located in another state, and all worthy of attention; so it came about that the entire family left their city home and moved far away to a cotton plantation. Tom and the girls went with the mother by steamer, while Joe, with the father and servants, went overland in patriarchal style, driving with them such flocks and herds as had accumulated on the little farm where our boys had spent the two summers mentioned.

In those days there was a little wheezy, rattling, ramshackle train that ran to Vicksburg, on the Mis-

sissippi river, and while, indeed, it was one of the sor-
riest outfits in America, it was an immense affair in
Tom's estimation. It passed every day in front of the
gate, but never, in his most reckless moment, did he
dare throw a clod of dirt at it, as he did at the plebeian
stage-coach, for vague rumors of little iron squirts, that
could throw streams of hot water to an incredible distance, had impressed all the boys with a most wholesome awe of this thing of smoke, and steam, and
wheels. That railway is one of the oldest in the United
States, and after being torn, twisted, and upheaved by
the angry veterans of Johnston and Grant, the traveler
glides over it in 'palace-cars upon well-ballasted steel
rails.

It was while the family were waiting at the depot
one cold December morning for the train to bear them
away upon their journey, our Tom picked up an idea
that was destined to bring him trouble in the near
future. A man came in to build a fire, and for lack of
a shovel he brought a live ember in his hands, which
he was enabled to do by passing it rapidly from one to
the other. This surprising performance captured Tom
and he mentally resolved that the first good chance he
would go and do likewise, but when he tried it he suddenly became a child of proverb. We never get over
learning by experience, and we drop many a hot coal
in the business of maturer years more readily than Tom
did in childhood.

At a tender age life in the city became a thing of the
past with our boys.

Suddenly, without a regret, they left the old home and plunged without remorse into the new realities of plantation life.

Tom went down the great Mississippi river on one of those wonderful floating palaces so famous in ante-bellum days for splendor, cards and explosions. The trip was a journey in wonderland, and everything from the mighty throb of the engine to the startling melody of the dinner-gong, that most diabolical of all contrivances for warning civilized man of his meal time, took our little man's fancy. So profound was the impression made upon his youthful mind by this trip that in after years, when at school, his first essay, or composition, barring a few animated nature descriptions of the dog, the cat, and the horse, was an account of the same.

A small boy called Johnnie was a fellow passenger of Tom's on that delightful trip, and soon became his most intimate chum. Together they explored all the dark corners of the boat and peered into mysterious places, or perched upon the never-absent cotton bale. Johnnie told how steamboats often "blowed up" and killed all the little boys; how dreadful snags lay in wait to " bust right into the side of the boat," and how big whales were out there in the water waiting to swallow the unfortunate people.

Tom listened to those awful stories until trembling at every revolution of the ponderous wheel he crept close to his little friend and declared in a whisper that he would not dare to sleep a wink that night. He for-

got all his fears when the stars came out and mother's
gentle arms bore him away to bed, and to childhood's
happy dreams.

Down the great river, past pretty towns and noble
plantations, towering bluffs—since become historical—
and willow-crowned points, the mighty steamer sped
until one gloomy morning she rounded to at a muddy
little town and Tom's river journey was ended for
many a year. This was his first trip upon the Mississippi, but not his last.   Let us see how it was that in
after years our hero so loved to travel on this same great
river, and how his hard-earned dollars went to buy coal
for a Mississippi steamboat.

When, on that first eventful journey, as Tom and
Johnnie were racing up and down the deck, getting in
everybody's way, there came down to the landing of a
great plantation a pretty little girl, with brown eyes
and curly hair. She came with her nurse to admire
the huge steamer, and as she shouted and clapped her
little hands, Tom and Johnnie cut their loftiest capers.
Was it fate? Tom is now sure that it was the work of
Providence, and kindly work, too.

The boat passed on its journey, the little girl faded
from view for many a year, to reappear in all the fresh
beauty of young womanhood, and we shall see Johnnie
no more. Many a time has Tom sat and pondered
over the fate of his vanished chum. Did he get
"blowed up," as he so often expressed it? Did he grow
tired of life's journey early and lie down by the way-
side to rest, or did he reach young manhood and then

give himself to his country upon some awful field of carnage? It is useless to speculate. Johnnie has served his purpose in this story, and since Tom has given him up for lost, from this good hour he shall be dead to us.

A muddy landing, where he lost one of his shoes, a long carriage ride through lanes, fields, and forests, over bridges and across fords, and Tom's first journey was ended, when, at supper-time, he found his first and only grandmama.

What a blessed name, and how we pity the boy or girl who never knew a grandmother! Dear, patient old mothers, who shield us so often from the righteous wrath of a parent, and whose store-room or pantry is always filled with goodies, how can I do you sufficient honor?

There is not a little girl in America who does not vow in her heart of hearts that she too will become a grand-mama, and there never was a man worthy of the name who would fail to take off his hat as one of these noble old mothers passed on her trembling way. Her dear face shines with angelic light, and heaven comes down to meet her as she draws near its portal. There is a halo of good deeds about the blessed head, and the restful song in her heart has never a note of discord.

CHAPTER III.

THE intelligent tourist when in Europe visits the house where Goethe was born, and wanders thoughtfully about the place that claims Dante; in America, the log cabin where Lincoln first saw the light, or the superb homes of Washington and Lee, are alike objects of untiring interest, but who will ever care to know anything about the early home of our Tom and our Joe? The house where they were born will never again echo to mortal footsteps, and we hope to tell in a later chapter how and when it ceased to be a habitation.

There was perhaps no lovelier or more homelike portion of America than the hill country of Eastern Louisiana, and it was well named by early settlers, "Happy land." Magnificent forests of hardwood, swift, purling streams through every valley, vast fields of corn and cotton, elegant residences and densely peopled quarters, all combined to make that favored section the one green spot of earth to thousands of happy dwellers. Enthusiastic men called it Paradise. Of one thing we are certain; during the decade ending with 1860 it was the beautiful Southland intensified, and the very home of contentment.

But the picture has changed as when upon some
summer day the tempest sweeps down a lovely valley
and blots out its fairest features.   Gone are its culti-
vated fields, its wealth, its customs, and forever gone
are most of its happy people.   The noble old men and
the tender old women who made Feliciana famous for
culture, and elegant hospitality, lived to see their wealth
all swept from them, and after a few years of toil and
sorrowing passed away.   The brave young men of that
region are scattered with the heroic dead on every battle-field from Manassas to Franklin, while the precious
girls have also vanished—"Some at the bridal and
some to the tomb."

Capital and labor may build again more costly homes
on every slope and forest-crowned hill; broader fields
may be opened, and the spring times that come and go
may bring back fairer flowers than those of the long
ago May-day; but no spring time, nor wealth, nor skill
and labor, can call again the happy peace and the
heavenly content that rested like a benediction upon
land and people.

It was in this lovely region and upon one of its noblest plantations that our two boys met to begin life
anew and drink in all its happy fullness for ten beautiful years.   Belhaven was a lovely home and its dwellers were content.   With a sturdy manliness, always his
characteristic, our Joe soon mastered every detail of
plantation life, and became his father's right-hand man.
Our fond eyes can see him yet, after thirty years, as
proudly conscious of the trust he carried the keys to

barn and storehouses, and superintended the distribution of rations for the servants or forage for the stock. Or, how confidently he rode into the neighboring village and looked after certain shipments of cotton, or selected sundry barrels of supplies. How readily the brave, thoughtful boy becomes the moving spirit of the farm, and how quickly all learn to rely upon him. His opinion is early sought in out-door matters and he has a voice in the family council. Blessed is the brave home boy in the eyes of father and mother, and to loving sisters he is the manliest man on earth.

Joe early became a mighty hunter, and took pleasure in initiating our little Tom into all the mysteries of both gun and rod. There is no happier mortal than a boy with a gun bringing down his first squirrel. After years may bring him many honors, much wealth, and an abundance of happiness, but we doubt if there is a more exquisite moment in all his career than this—when, unheeding the misery inflicted upon a poor little creature, bang goes the gun, and down comes the game. How intimately our pleasures are often blended with the suffering of some other creature, and some of our joys are builded upon the sorrows of a fellow!

Tom used to be Joe's shadow, and went with him always to "turn the squirrels" and carry the game nor will he ever forget the occasion, or the place, when finding two large fox-squirrels in one tree, Joe generously allowed him to choose one and take a shot at it. So important an event in Tom's career must have, as it deserves, more than a passing notice. We know the spot well, for did Tom ever pass it without calling attention to his exploit! Never. Yes, he did go by once, a few years later, but he was in an awful hurry and did not linger. Later on we will tell why Tom was so interested in getting away from there.

The tree where this squirrel episode took place was a pine to which clung a large muscadine vine, and it probably yet stands at the foot of a rocky hill near the old pasture-field of Belhaven. The gun was a long double-barreled fowling piece, famous in all that section for its shooting qualities, but so heavy that it required almost a man's strength to handle it. There was no kinder brother than Joe, so he humped his back and let Tom take a rest on it, until after a long and tiresome effort to get aim there came a tremendous bang and the sad little period of one squirrel's life was forever rounded. Intensely excited, Tom dropped the gun, gathered up the game, and almost flew to the house, a mile away, where admiring mother and sisters listened with unflagging interest to every detail of the killing and foretold greater things for the future. The Judge also took great interest in his son's performance, for he was himself an accomplished sportsman, and ordered an extra quantity of lightwood prepared in case it became necessary to sit up with Tom that night.

"You are making fun of me now, father," cried the boy, and his eyes began to fill, when just then Joe came in, and in his affectionate way told again the wonderful story until Tom was too proud to cry.

Since that day the young Nimrod has brought down all sorts and sizes of game with the latest improved tackle, but never again will he kill his first squirrel, and alas! alas! poor, dear, generous Joe will never again applaud the successful hunter.

Those blessed days and years that fled all too quickly at beautiful Belhaven measured the time until 1861.

Tom was then twelve years of age and Joe was seventeen—still brothers, always companions. At school together, and side by side in the cotton-patch; roaming the beech-covered hills, plunging into the neighboring swimming hole, hunting the coon and opossum during the stilly hours of night, or watching the winter flight of duck and pigeon; always together, our two boys looked only to a happy future, and dreamed of no sorrow so great as separation.

We cling to those we love, but a mightier power—call it Fate or Providence—drags us asunder, and as we drift apart in clouds and darkness, poor mute hands beckon to each other through the mist.

Our boys had lived in an Eden, and saw not the shadow just over the wall. The quiet corner where they grew in strength and happiness was as free from care as the home of our first parents, but by-and-by they heard vague rumors of two great serpents, called Abolition and Secession, which were filling all the land with the sound of their hissings, so that men began to assemble and discuss the prospect, or possibilities, of some dreadful political convulsion. In the light of to-day it seems strange that there was no Hercules powerful enough to strangle those dread ministers of Fate, but men were mad and reason had fled away. The accumulated wrath of many a bitter controversy had filled their hearts and nerved their arms for a struggle to the death. The demon in man was unloosed for a season, and brothers who had followed the starry flag to freedom and to fame forgot that they were brothers.

All was love and peace at Belhaven, but the deluge came, and the song of birds was heard no more. What could our two boys know of such things? and it was cruel to break in upon their happy lives. It seemed cruel then, and it seems cruel now. Perhaps one day we shall all know why it was permitted.

CHAPTER IV.

BOY HEAVEN.

THE boy who does not love to fish, if one such exists, will bear watching. There is something wrong in his make-up; some inherent lack of naturalness that calls for our pity rather than our condemnation. The sport may be called cruel, but we shall not discuss that question, nor shall we point out the numberless laws and authorities justifying it, from the day when the apostle said "I go a-fishing," until now. We will only accept a delightful fact, and continue to dig for earthworms when the flowers blossom and the birds mate. We are really sorry for the boy who takes no pleasure in fishing. He is not fairly rounding out life's joys, and passes into manhood without knowing all the capabilities of boyhood. The twelve-year-old boy finds more genuine pleasure fishing for mudcats, eels, and suckers, along some dirty little creek, than grown-up folks can ever know amid clearer waters and more royal game.

Our Tom and Joe loved to fish. They were earnest sportsmen and intensely natural, hence it was that one fine spring morning in 1861 Joe bounced out of bed and called:

"Tom! Tom! get up, you lazy young rascal!"

"Oh, go away, Joe! I'm sleepy," answered Tom, then he yawned and stretched, rolling over for another nap. Joe again called: "Tom! come now, be lively, and listen to the birds. I hear the red-bird and the joree fairly splitting their little throats out in the front woods. Get up, boy, get up! Out with you, and hear them!"

"Oh, plague on the birds, let 'em split! I'll fling a rock at them when I get out. Why the diccance can't you let a fellow sleep?"—then the young sluggard turned over to the wall.

But Joe persisted—"I say, Tom! I saw the dogwood along the spring branch all bursting out into bloom yesterday."

"Well, what of it? Confound it all, Joe! here you are first bothering me about the birds, and now poking your flowers at me! Can't you let them bloom in peace? What do you suppose I care for all the dogwood wood blossoms this side of Halifax? Git out with you!"

Tom was now thoroughly mad, and covering his head with the pillow, determined to hear no more, but Joe laughingly replied:

"All right, young man. I thought you knew that when the dogwood blooms it is time for trout to bite. I am going fishing after breakfast, but you may stay at home."

At the first mention of fish Tom was wide-awake, and drawing his head from under the cover, where he had thrust it, sprang out of bed with a bounce.

"Hurrah for General Jackson!" he shouted, "we are going fishing! we are going fishing!" and as he

2

crawled into his trousers he rattled away: "I was
down at the creek yesterday, when father sent me to
look for the big spotted sow, that has eight cunning
little pigs, and I thought the water looked awful nice
and fishy. Shall I dig some worms for perch and minnows, Joe? There's just oodles of worms, great, long,
wriggling fellows, out back of the wash-shed, and I can
get a gourdful in most no time."

"All right," replied Joe, " you get the bait and I'll look
after the hooks and lines, which need overhauling.
Go by mother's room and ask her to hurry the cook
with breakfast. I talked with father last night and
wanted him to go with us, but he has to go to town
to-day on business, so we must go without him. You
dig the bait quickly, and run drive the calves to the
pasture; as soon as I look over these fishing lines I will
get old Pedro and carry a bag of cotton-seed up to the
big mud hole for the hogs, and by that time breakfast
will be ready."

Our boys sped away whistling and shouting upon
the mission of their several farm duties, and soon after
sunrise, with breakfast hastily swallowed, well-filled
lunch-basket, gourdful of earth worms and grubs, off
they went to spend a day in the forest, and along the
bank of the bright little creek. O, beautiful day! O,
day of perfect joy! day to be remembered while Tom
lives, and we doubt not that in the hereafter the unfor-
getting spirit will fondly dwell upon it, and recall its
pleasures for comparison with nobler joys!

In front of the dwelling at Belhaven is one of the noblest forests of magnolia, oak, beech, and sweetgum that ever delighted human eye, while the surface sweeps gradually and beautifully down for about one third of a mile to a little spring branch at the edge of what was called the swamp.

The boys sped rapidly through that beautiful grove, then on for a few hundred yards underneath the heavy timber of the swamp, across the "slashes" by a mighty foot-log, they followed a well-beaten path amid swamp laurel and pawpaw thickets to the creek. Here was one of the famous fishing and swimming holes, known to all the boys of the neighborhood, which Tom and Joe now approached with quiet footsteps, and with breathless alacrity prepared for the day's sport.

"Now, Tom, you put your small hook over in the shallow water near the sand bar and catch me a shiner. I think there is a trout at the riffle where the water passes over that log, and with a nice live bait I can catch him."

"Oh, Joe, catch your own minnows! I want to catch a perch here at this little drift,"—and our unobliging young fisherman, seating himself upon a mossy beech root, at once forgot how much kindness he owed to Joe.

"Tom, you are a mean, chuckle-headed fellow, and are awfully unobliging. You forget that I pummelled John Barton not long ago for slapping you, although you richly deserved a licking. John says you put

cockleburrs under his saddle and made old Prince run
away with him, and that you chopped his shinny-stick
into pieces with the axe. Of course you deserved a
thrashing, as you do about three times a day, but then
he is not the fellow to give it to you. So now after all
this, you wont oblige me? Suppose I catch a fine
trout? you will be the very first one at the table to
want a piece of it." Joe nearly lost his temper with
his little brother this time and Tom fired in with—

"That's all very well for you to say, Joe, but you
know that mother always eats the trout, and for my
part I'd rather have blue cat any day."

He saw the pained expression on Joe's face and his
conscience smote him, for his kind brother was very
dear to Tom, so he said: " Forgive me, Joe, dear. It was
mighty good of you to wallop old John Barton, the old
pug-nosed rascal! He took his great foot and kicked
all my marbles out of the ring, off into the grass, so I
lost my pretty agate that father bought me Christmas,
and that cute little black alley. I despise him! I could
beat him half to death—but I'll get even with him if
it takes me a thousand years."

" I'll catch you a minnow, Joe, and I'm sorry I was so
selfish—besides, the perch don't bite here worth
shucks."

There seems to have been a good deal of every-day
human nature about our Tom. The perch refused to
bite, so he became very penitent and was ready to give
up his own pleasure to wait upon his brother. It often
happens that way with older persons when perch refuse

to bite. Ere long a bright, dancing silverside was dangling on the end of Tom's line, and hooking it carefully under the dorsal fin, Joe had as pretty a bait as ever tempted the fastidious trout from his lair beneath beech roots.

All was now suppressed excitement while Joe played his minnow to attract the royal game. Tom scarcely dared to breathe, and an ill-timed sneeze would have sent him to execution at once. The bright waters rippled and sang their lullaby over fallen tree and bended reed; an early kingfisher, intent upon his breakfast, plunged from a neighboring bough upon a luckless minnow; the cat bird called to its mate in the alder bushes around the bend, and the Spanish bugler, whose mellow notes along the creek always indicate good fishing, was piping his sweetest, when suddenly there came a splash—a gleam of white flashed with the rapidity of lightning—then away went Joe's cork, and his line fairly whizzed through the water.

"Ge-e-e-mennie, what a whopper! Hold him, Joe! Jerk him out!" cried Tom, but our Joe was older and wiser. He had learned that the most exquisite joy of the angler is not in yanking his game suddenly upon the bank, but in allowing it to play; in feeling the electric thrill that passes along the line and rod; in conquering the noble fish gently and skillfully. Away went the line, singing through the water, until it was perfectly taut and the pliant rod was bent like a bow. "Easy, now, old fellow," said Joe, "you'll not get under those roots if I can help it. Play now until you are

tired, and—wup, sir!" as the fish sprang wildly out of
the water trying in vain to shake the hook from its
mouth. "Gracious! he'll get loose if he does that
again." The angler was skillful and the fish was
game, but the odds were all on one side, and soon the
noble trout gave up the struggle, floundering helplessly
upon its side, until it was gently drawn to the bank
and cast fluttering upon the leaves.

"He is a good one, and will weigh at least three
pounds," cried the exultant Joe, as he looked with a
fisherman's pride upon his catch.

"Three pounds!" answered Tom. "Three diccance!
I'll bet you a thousand dollars it will weigh ten pounds
on any scale that ever was invented. Three pounds,
indeed! I'd like to see mother try to eat all that fish.
She will have to call in father and the girls to help
her. I'll call it ten pounds, anyhow." Thus we see
our Tom beginning early to lay the foundation for his
future fame as a manufacturer of fish stories. The boy
could not keep away from the big fish, but sadly neglected his own hook, until an exclamation from Joe:

"Look out, Tom! something has got your line, and
is running off with it." Greatly excited, Tom sprang
to reach his pole, when a wild honeysuckle tripped his
foot, and he rolled down the slope, heels over head,
landing near the water's edge in exactly the right
place. Seizing his rod, he gave it a mighty jerk, landing hook, line, and fish twenty feet above, among the
limbs of the old beech at whose base he had been sitting.

"You seem to be in a hurry!" laughed Joe.

"Oh, pshaw! dog-bite such luck!" exclaimed Tom, whose face was the living image of despair. "I wish you would look at that, Joe. Now, ain't that enough to make a fellow cuss? Just look what a fish! It's all mouth, as father said of that fellow we heard talking about the Yankees the other day, at the big meeting in town. He said he could whip five Yankees any day, and that he would undertake to drink all the blood shed in the war people are talking about. You think he could do it, Joe?"

Tom had caught one of those funny-looking perch whose development of mouth is something marvelous.

Joe answered him that the wild-talking man would probably not fight so well as he talked, then with infinite patience he untangled the line from the tree, and all was lovely again. Some beautiful speckled perch, a half-dozen red-horses, as many black bream, rewarded Joe's skill, but nothing more like the champion trout. Tom caught several small sunfish, a couple of idiotic suckers, and finally wound up the afternoon by hauling out a magnificent blue-cat, the king of all game fish in Southern waters. Such wonderful sport they had that day, and what a glorious appetite! They could hardly wait until the great bell of a neighboring plantation rang out the hour of twelve, to attack the well-filled lunch basket. Boys get hungry early and often; especially is this true when off in the woods on a day of frolic. No other pleasure can overshadow the anticipation of dinner, unless it be the dinner, and the afternoon reflections, when, lying upon a mossy knoll

near the creek, gazing contentedly at the distant blue
that glimmers down amid the overhanging branches,
are a species of bliss not to be ignored in this prosaic
world of ours.

The young fishermen were hungry, and the dinner
was most enticing.   What delicious, home-cured ham !
and there never was such bread as the old-time sweet-
potato biscuit that Aunt Viney, the cook, used to make
at Belhaven !   Eggs, hard boiled, and a little paper of
pepper and salt.   No dyspepsia troubled those two
sturdy country boys, and later on, one dreadful night
upon the battle-field of Chickamauga, Joe ate seventeen
hard-boiled eggs to nerve him for the next day's fearful conflict.   But the basket is not yet empty.   Those
slices of potato-pone, spiced and browned until fit for a
king, or an American citizen, still cling to Tom's memory.   He has partaken of many noble banquets since
that day ; has dined at the fashionable restaurants of
our great cities ; partaken of unlimited wedding cake,
and enjoyed the steak of venison when hunger was
sharpened by keen mountain air, but never with such
a relish as when a boy on the old plantation he wrestled
with the toothsome potato-pone.   Yet there are thousands of persons in this vast country who never heard
of that dish, and tens of thousands who never tasted.
We are sorry for them.   Perhaps Tom's boyish appetite
doesn't linger with him until now.   He always swears,
gastronomically, by Aunt Viney, and declares that the
Roman Emperor who knighted a subject for inventing
a new dish would have made her an Ethiopic queen.

Such a day and such a dinner! Two joyous happy boys in boy heaven! Yet even as they lolled along the banks of the creek singing and shouting in all the abandon of young life, or lingered above the clear waters dreaming such dreams as come only to happy boyhood, the long-peaceful land was startled by the explosion of great guns, and from out the sulphurous clouds that hung over Charleston harbor leaped lightnings whose deadly glare was destined to blind the eyes and reason of raging millions. The bells were wildly ringing in all great cities a tocsin that would soon be muffled into a funeral knell. No sound reached the two happy boys, for they were out in the forest with nature and close to the God of nature.

As Tom and Joe stepped into the house that evening they met their father, who had just returned from town.

"Boys," said he, quivering with excitement, "the war has begun. The Confederates opened fire on Fort Sumter this morning. Oh, my God! what is to become of our poor country!"

CHAPTER V.

AN ORIGINAL UNION MAN.

THERE was a strange commingling of joy and sorrow all over the South on that fateful night of April 12th, 1861. Thousands were rejoicing that the decisive step had been taken, and yet other thousands were full of grief when they remembered the dear old flag that was then waving grandly as of old, amid a storm of shot and shell. Every intelligent boy in the land had dreamed of heroic endeavor under that flag, and many brave men of the South looked to it with love and hope amid the tempest of battle in far off Mexico.

By a bare majority had the State of Louisiana voted to leave the Federal Union, and among the many thousands who loved that Union, and its glorious banner, none were more honest in devotion than the father of our boys. After supper, where mother had made an heroic effort to eat the trout, as Tom had predicted, and he had feasted on blue-cat, the family all assembled in the sitting-room to discuss the mighty event of that day. Joe had read the newspapers and kept pace with the drift of events so that his mind was made up. Every boy in the South who reached the age of seventeen prior to the war knew a great deal about the political history of his country. They read the papers, and got their political bias from some one of the great journals of the age. Quick to argue a point, or dispute a proposition, they were born politicians.

"Father," said Joe, "I tried to-day while we were fishing to explain to Tom why Louisiana and the other Southern States have a perfect right to secede, but he is so pig-headed that he won't understand it. I think the young rascal is a half abolitionist anyhow."

"It's no such of a thing!" wrathfully cried Tom; "but I don't want to belong to any other country than the good old United States, and I should like to know what is going to become of George Washington and Andrew Jackson if we go off and make a new country?"

"We will take their bones along with us if that will do any good," replied Joe; "besides, Tennessee and Virginia are bound to come. But, father, give us your views, and may be you can settle the young man."

There was a solemn pause for a few moments, and such a hush fell on the assembly as comes over a court-room when the judge puts on the black cap; then in low tones the father proceeded to tell what he thought of the momentous question.

"My son, you all know that two weeks ago I voted against Secession, and I prayed as I voted. I thought it not only inexpedient, but wrong. I am a whig, and I love the Union as Mr. Clay loved it; but I am also a believer in the wholesome democratic doctrine of majority rule. My State, exercising her sovereign will, has gone out of the Union, and now I have no choice but to cling to her, however my views may differ from those of the majority. The king can do no wrong, and my State is my king. I yet think that secession is wrong in practice, since we have no just cause for leaving the Federal Union. There has been no violation of the constitution, nor can I see where any established right of ours has been legally restricted. True it is that they hide our runaway slaves up North beyond the reach of the authorities, and it may be that the authorities do not try to find them, but we on the other hand hang such fellows as we catch here meddling with our negroes, so the honors are about even.

"We have fuller representation in Congress than the non-slaveholding States, inasmuch as our slaves, who cannot vote, are in fact represented. That we did not vote for Mr. Lincoln was our privilege, and it was equally the privilege of our Northern brethren to vote for him. They did vote for him and he was legally elected. What reason have we for complaining? We scattered our votes among three candidates and so lost them all, therefore, we should abide the result of our folly. This very fact shows how hopelessly we are divided in the presence of the gravest political movement of the age; and let me say further, that there can be no adverse legislation that will trample the constitutional rights of any section, or individual, for we have a Supreme Court which has been uniformly friendly to us and our pet institution. Should we cling to the government our strength in Congress will prevent any very hostile legislation; and there is sufficient friendly sentiment in the Northern States to keep us from all harm if we are found at our post. Furthermore, the government and the flag are ours as much as they belong to any other section, but when we thrust these things from us, and disclaim all interest in both; when we violate the law and resist the authority of that government, we need not expect anything else than trouble. We of Louisiana, especially, have no right to secede, for did not the United States buy us with their money, making us one of the family, and when we were threatened with foreign invasion sent that great soldier and ardent Unionist, Andrew Jackson, by whom all democrats swear, to protect us? Even our boy Tom there knows how well he did it. We were purchased from a European despotism, and made a sovereign state, so you see, my son, it is the rankest ingratitude for us to destroy the mother who took us to her bosom and nurtured us."

Joe here interrupted: "But, father, do not many of the ablest expounders of the constitution declare that under the compact the right of withdrawal was never surrendered, and consequently any State is at perfect liberty to withdraw from the Union?"

"Yes, my son, many very learned men take that position, yet I think they are wrong. We are all very apt to construe an instrument to accord with our own desires, hence we are rarely free from bias. I love the Union and am prejudiced that way. I do not believe that you can anywhere find that the right of withdrawal was reserved to the States, hence it must have been surrendered for the mutual good. It is more than likely that the patriots of old never contemplated such a state of affairs as now confronts us

"But suppose we grant that a State has the right to secede, I still hold such an act to be both unwise and inexpedient. The American Union is a result of the loftiest patriotism and the sublimest human wisdom, but if that Union may be dissolved at the pleasure of one of the contracting parties, then it is a stupendous monument of human folly. No, my children, the founders of this government never contemplated any other than a united people. Even should we succeed in this mad attempt we will only have destroyed the noblest form of government ever devised by man. No good can result to us, nor can we expect any degree of permanency. We are forming a Southern Confederacy which is only the realization of a political dream, but what will hold these States together, do you suppose? Texas, Arkansas, and Missouri will form a confederacy west of the Mississippi river in less than ten years, and will force Western Louisiana to go with them, making a boundary of the great river and looking to New and Old Mexico for more territory. Secession will prove a contagious disease.

"What is there to hold us together but slavery? and I thank God, my children, that this curse will soon be removed. It has proven a terrible misfortune to us, but the institution is surely doomed. How can it stand when opposed by the civilized world? Every relic of barbarism is rapidly disappearing in the light of this century, and human slavery must go.

"Again I say, secession is inexpedient, because, be it never so lawful, it is doomed to failure should the government undertake to coerce us. This same government which is ours will, since we disown it, backed by the powerful North, and confronted only by a divided people, compel us by force to return into the fold. The boom of cannon this morning at Charleston has sounded our death-knell, and as Mr. Stephens, of Georgia, in a wonderful speech recently told his people, we shall feel the shock of contending armies and all the wild desolations of war. I believe his to be a prophecy—a prophecy of evil indeed, but true as the woes foretold of Jerusalem."

"So, father, you think the Yankees will thrash us, do you?" cried Joe.

"Yes, my son, they will if they try, and I think that after to-day's wild work they will try."

"Very well," replied the impulsive boy, "let them try! I think we are right, and we will make each hill-side a battle-field until every valley is a graveyard."

"Hurrah for Joe and the Southern Confederacy!" shouted Tom. "Let us start for Fort Sumter early in the morning, Joe. Father, let me have your shotgun, and Joe can take the rifle. I'll ride Don Pedro, and Joe can ride young Buchanan, so we'll be cavalry. Mother, I wish you would sew some red stripes on my pants to-night, and put Dora's new ostrich plume in my hat."

"Never mind, Tom—don't get in too big a hurry. If you go off to the war who will drive up the cows? We cannot spare you yet awhile, my boy, and if you go off with such a rush I would like to know who will tie up that big toe that you knock against every stump in your path."

This cruel cut was from mother, and reminded Tom that he was not yet a dashing cavalryman, but only a small boy with a sore toe. That night Tom dreamed that he led a great cavalry charge against Fort Sumter and fell desperately wounded in the toe.

There was not much sleeping at Belhaven that night, except among the children, and we doubt not that all over this broad land, both North and South, good men and women, were unable to sleep for thinking of the dreadful drama upon which the curtain was then rising. Well might they be restless, for the demon was unloosed and the tempest was driving on that would vex men's souls, and wreck the fairest hopes of many a happy home. "The State can do no wrong, and I must go with my State," sighed the good old Judge.

The next morning, under a pretense of going hunting, Joe and Tom went away up to the old field pasture and practiced at long range with the rifle upon a great oak that stood, and yet stands, on the hillside. Twenty years later, Tom stood at the foot of the old oak and looked, with tear-dimmed eyes, upon the scars of that day's marksmanship. He went to the spot where our young soldiers stood and tried to see the target, but the wild and tangled growth had sprung up as dense as that which shuts off the view of the opposing lines in front of Petersburg. As the tender memory of those vanished years swept over him, from the great deep of his heart came this plaint:

"Oh, Joe, Joe! would to God you could come back to me, and you and I were boys again, fighting the mimic war or casting our lines for the wary trout. And oh, dear, patriotic old father! although the coffin-lid has hidden the light of thine earthly crown of glory, thou hast a crown immortal."

CHAPTER VI.

"THEY MARCHED AWAY DOWN THE VILLAGE STREET."

OUR boys never went fishing together again. The bright waters, the birds, and the forest wooed them in vain, for all interest now centered in town. There gaily dressed officers were persuading the young men to enlist for a six month's term in the army then being formed, nor indeed was any persuasion necessary. Never in the history of war did men respond more cheerfully, and the better class of Southern youths in 1861 could not be excelled in enthusiasm and determined courage. Filled to overflowing with the wild spirit of adventure, and imbued with ideas of old-time chivalry, they hungered for renown. The best blood of the land was on fire ; the pride of the people was appealed to as it had never been before, and every college sent forth a company. The young men of wealth and intelligence enlisted at once, all fearing lest the war should end ere they could win the glory that would crown them heroes in after life. They were wild with enthusiasm, and called it patriotism. It became patriotism later on, when, with heroic fortitude worthy of success, they toiled and hungered, suffered and died. One of the most pitiful pictures the world ever beheld was the suffering and death of those noble boys, battling for a political idea, and glorifying it forever; hallowing it with a love of country immortal as the sufferings at Valley Forge. We believe as we are educated. They fought as they had been taught from the cradle, and made heroic history. The unvarnished facts of their mighty endeavor compel recognition through all the ages, and criticism is disarmed in the presence of their tremendous struggle. The mounds formed over their unknown graves have long ago been levelled with the earth, and many of those who waited and wept for them have little grass-covered mounds of their own—all forgotten by the busy world. Will you forget them, oh, suffering Southland! Never, never. We love them for their heroic lives and their glorious death. We must tell our children the story, and teach them to uncover when they pass the lonely grave of a Confederate soldier.

Our two boys dropped their books, neglected the pigs, ignored the cows, and bade the squirrels wait until the frolic was over. Tom even forgot Robinson Crusoe, and left him scared almost to death over the savage track, while he went off to look for other tracks which were beginning to impress the sand upon every shore—tracks that were destined to mark the sweep of desolation all over the fair land and be filled with blood.

Early in the month of May the second company was being formed in the town of Clinton, and every afternoon, at the public square, the band would play

patriotic music, then impassioned orators would take
up the theme and paint, in beautiful word-pictures, the
"path of glory." Alas! that the canvass should
shadow the grave! One day, after several stirring
talks and the crash of warlike music, a call was made
for volunteers. Captain Hargrove, a dignified, sol-
dierly-looking gentleman, announced that he held a
commission authorizing him to raise a company in that
town, and that he was ready to enroll the names of all
who felt it their duty to arm in defence of their native
land. He told the assembled crowd that the war was
becoming a serious thing, and whilst the call was made
for six months only, the probabilities were that troops
would be needed longer. He stated, further, that the
indications all justified the belief that the Federal
Government really meant to coerce the seceded States
and compel their return into the Union.

"Shall we," said the speaker, "remain at home
in ease while our brethren in Virginia are standing a living wall against the invaders? Can it be
said that the men of Louisiana are slow to meet danger? Will they shrink from the path to glory and
honor? Never! never! When duty calls, no true
son of the South ever yet failed to go. Every heroic
tradition of the past, and every glorious hope for the
future, appeals to us in the voice of our country; then
together let us seek the foe and give him battle."

A mighty shout of approval greeted the words of the
speaker, and on that day the "rebel yell," destined to
electrify the fighting spirits of all future ages, was born.

With a hurrah the boys crowded to the speaker's stand and gave their names for membership. Eighty-seven noble young men responded to the call, and seventh upon the list was the name of Joseph Mabry. Tom was present and went wild with enthusiasm. He heard the thrilling words, such as he had read in books of history; he saw floating above him a banner with a strange new device; he saw before him a noble uniform of grey, which will forever symbolize marvelous courage and heroic endurance; then straightway he forgot the old banner that he loved and became a rebel. When he saw Joe go forward a wild impulse seized him to go and be a soldier, too. The impulse of manhood came upon him, and forgetting the cows and pigs that were awaiting his return home to Belhaven, forgetting the hunting and fishing, forgetting father and mother, he rushed to the stand and begged for the privilege of going with Joe. It was pathetic to hear him plead for a trial, and see him tiptoe to make believe that he carried the stature of a man.

"My God!" exclaimed old Major Chatham, a veteran of 1812, "are our babies going to this inhuman war?"

Had the old soldier lived to the end, he would have seen boyish limbs mangled by shot and shell, and the "seed-corn of the Confederacy" buried on many a bloody hillside.

Captain Hargrove, with all the gentleness of a father, put his hand on Tom's shoulder and told him to come around to his office when the meeting adjourned to

talk the matter over   The boy went home that evening silent, but unconvinced.   It took an awful shock to
silence him in those days.   He had played, hunted,
fished, worked and schooled with Joe, nor could he see
any just cause why they might not fight together.

Great was the consternation **at** home that night
when they learned that **Joe** had **become** a soldier.
Father and mother **gave their** consent, although he
was only seventeen; but Dora, the brown-eyed sister
next in age **to Joe**, rebelled and vowed she would do
something awful, until **Tom** interfered and told her
that in case she seceded from the family he would be
compelled to coerce her into submission.   "Secession"
and "coercion" were household words at that time, and
our Tom was just the boy to turn the most solemn text
into slang.   All was now preparation for the departure
of the young soldier.   There were so many things to
arrange, and so many busy hands to assist in the labor
of love; but all the while the aged father **went** about
his daily affairs with a heavy heart, for he knew that
his darling boy was going away to endure great suffering, and may be to die.   The two weeks allowed to
make ready for the start soon sped, and now on the day
before the last night to be spent at home, Joe and Tom
walked about over the farm, and talked of the happy
past, or dwelt upon a glowing future.   As they walked
they communed as only two loving brothers can.

"I must go back into the big pasture once more, Tom,
and climb again into the great mulberry tree—they
must be ripe now—and I want to see the old plum-

thicket in the valley of the sedge-field once more. It is getting quite warm, and I should enjoy a loll under the shade of the three large sweetgums that stand in a clump on dead-horse hill. Suppose we go by and see if the chinquapen is in bloom, and we can try our skill in jumping across Blackberry run just below the water-gate, as we used to do. That old pasture where we have loitered so often picking blackberries and search-ing for the cows is very dear to me, and now I feel that I may never look upon it again. The persimmon thicket, where we caught the two 'possums one night last fall, and that queer circle of cottonwoods, must be visited before I go. All the little details of the old life, now that I am about to leave it, come back to me, Tom, with a clearness that makes me wonder, and the desire to cling to them is almost a burden. I know now how the poor exile must feel when leaving his native land forever. And Tom, my brother, sometime when I am gone, when I am far away, I want you to see Jennie and tell her that I could not bid her good-bye. Tell her that I shall dream of her by the camp-fires and in the dread day of battle I shall prove to her that I am not a coward. She thinks that I am faint-hearted because I refused to fight John Barton last February at the Valentine party, and declares that she will never smile on me again. She will not understand my motive in refusing to fight, but some day I trust she will know me better. Tell her that I forgive her cruel words, and that I shall love her even unto death, believing that she will be sorry when she appreciates the truth. I have learned in the last twelve months, Tom, that God does not love the brawler and the stirrer up of strife, hence I cannot fight John Barton, on my own account, unless compelled. You know that I am not afraid of him, and you recollect well that I thrashed him not long since on your behalf."

Tom promised, but he was not satisfied. "I tell you what, Joe, I wouldn't fret about Jennie, with her snappish eyes and pretty face. She is awful sweet when she wants to be, but she ain't half good enough for you. I wouldn't mind about giving old John Barton another walloping, either, if I were you. Hang me, if I don't do it myself when I get a little older. You talk about the Bible being opposed to fighting; why, boy, it's made up of rows and battles, and I find the book of Kings about as interesting as the 'Conquest of Mexico,' or the history of Robert Bruce. Wasn't Samson a whale, though? But, Joe, I'll tell Jennie, if you say so, and I'll tell her that when you come back a colonel she shan't have you. I'll bet a thousand dollars that you won't notice her when you are on General Beauregard's staff."

Tom did not forget Joe's instructions, and we are afraid that he did not mend matters any. His intentions were good, and he championed Joe so enthusiastically, so much to the disparagement of the young lady herself, that he almost got his face slapped for his pains.

Until late afternoon of this last day did our boys wander about the plantation and visit all the pleasant spots. They talked and communed as only two loving brothers can, and Tom made a world of promises how he would care for young Buchanan, and rub him down daily. Six months later, to the boy's intense disgust, the good pony was "pressed," and became the property of a Confederate cavalryman.

Around the family circle the members all lingered that night, until, at a late hour, the altar was erected, and amid the tears of love and sorrow, prayers for the young soldier went up beyond the stars to Him who heareth and answereth prayer in His own appointed way.

Early in the morning Joe was up, dressed in his smart uniform, and ready to start. Going into the sitting-room, he found the Judge at the table, leaning his head upon his hands, apparently just as he was when the good-nights were said.

"Why, father, you are up early—you look weary."

"Yes, my son. I did not go to bed at all. I could not sleep, and here I have prayed for you all night."

"Oh, my father!" was all Joe could say, as they were clasped in each other's arms. Other farewells were said in the rooms of mother and sisters, too tender for words, then came the old family servants to say good-bye to "Marse Joe." Uncle Zeb, the foreman, was spokesman for the party, and with tears in his eyes, the faithful old man faltered:

"May de Lord God A'mighty bless you, Marse Joe, an' keep you in de holler of His han'! You is been a good young marster to us all, and we all gwinter miss

3

you when you gone. We all luv you, Marse Joe, an' we gwinter pray fer you constant."

"Good-bye, honey," sobbed Aunt Viney, "dese old arms dun nussed you many a time. Don't forgit your 'ligion, chile, and look to de King when tribulations come."

Joe's tears flowed afresh as he bade the faithful negroes farewell, and now at the front gate, holding young Buchanan, ready saddled, was Tom, and the boy who was going along to lead the horse back.

"I've tended to Buck well for you, Joe, and now he is all ready. Oh, Joe, Joe! why can't I go, too? All the boys are going, and here I am yet a baby. They had better put me in long dresses at once, and feed me out of a bottle, and I am getting so long-legged, too, that I am ashamed to stay at home. Why, I'm twelve years old now—next year I'll be thirteen, and I bet you a thousand dollars I'll go then, if I have to run away! Why, Joe, Andrew Jackson was only thirteen years old when he fought in the battle of the Waxhaws, and everybody is proud of him. He was an orphan and could have his own way; it does look like some boys have all the luck."

Thus wailed Tom at being compelled to remain away from the wars—and the silly boy did not know that there were numbers of men who would have given a small fortune for his excuse.

"My dear Tom, you must be reasonable," answered Joe, "and you must listen to father. Now, I want you to make me one last promise—listen, Tom, and promise, won't you?"

"Yes, dear old Joe, yes, yes. Anything for your sake," answered the boy.

"Well, my little brother, I want you to stay at home until father gives you permission to leave. The dear old folks will need you, and you are worth more to them than to your country."

"Oh, Joe! That is mighty hard, and will ruin me forever, for they never will consent, and I'll be called a coward or a stay-at-home. Joe, you are ruining my life."

"Never mind, Tom. It is mighty hard to do our duty sometimes, but I have your promise, and I know you will keep it—so, good-bye, my own brave little brother; may God bless you, and make you a good man!"

There, when the first flush of sunrise gilded the top of the mighty beeches in front of Belhaven, the brothers parted, and never sunrise witnessed parting more tender. In a perfect tempest of grief Tom threw himself into Joe's arms, and clung to him until the latter, gently disengaging himself, mounted his horse and rode slowly down the avenue. Tom watched him until a turn in the road hid both horse and rider, then, with a passionate longing to see his brother once more, he ran across the field by a near cut, and hiding in the sedge by the old negro graveyard, saw Joe ride slowly past, and heard his clear tenor voice singing:

"I dream of Jennie, and my heart bows low,
  Never more to meet her where the wild waters flow."

CHAPTER VII.

THE DEAD ROLL OF SHILOH.

WHO can tell how sad and lonesome our Tom was when the farewells had been said! All that day, and for many days thereafter, he wandered about the farm, and seemed to be looking for something he could never find; nor did he rouse from that listless condition until there came a long letter from Joe, telling all about his new life in the camp of instruction. The company had been incorporated into a regiment, and, with many others, had pitched their tents for a short season at Camp Moore, in the pine hills of eastern Louisiana. Here they drilled and frolicked, sang and danced, as if it were indeed a picnic—yet all the while complaining that they had no taste of war. Oh! could they have foreseen the horrors which awaited them, or caught but one glimpse of the bloody stream that must flow until all the land was in mourning! It is a kindly ordering of Providence that shuts out the future from our knowledge, and we move on through life, singing for very joy, until suddenly the end comes. Better for us to sing and carry a laughing face, with a light heart, for the end will come, be we sad or gay. The man who laughs—we mean the man whose laugh is pleasant and natural—is always welcome. Even if

we know him to be a rascal, we to a certain extent forgive him for the pleasure he bestows; at all events, we
don't cross over to the other side of the street when we
see him a block away.

Tom's parents appealed to him to cheer up, and take
Joe's place on the farm. The poor fellow did his best,
and, assuming the duties of that position, his old-time
cheerfulness returned; he became manlier and more
thoughtful, was more considerate of others, and in
short—this assumption of responsibility did by Tom as
it does by nine out of ten boys—made a man of him.
He gave up going barefooted about this time, although
he dearly loved a freedom from the tyranny of shoe
leather, and he avers to this day that there are few
pleasures more exquisite than making barefoot tracks
in the newly-plowed soil. There is nothing esthetic
in such pleasures. They are " of the earth, earthy."

Our young man did not quit off permanently,
although he made repeated trials, until one afternoon
upon a neighborhood road he was suddenly captured by
a party of mischievous girls under the leadership of Jennie, who badgered him unmercifully until his barefeet
were almost as crimson as his face. The girls were too
lady-like to seem to notice the absence of Tom's shoes but
he missed them, and would have swapped his hopes of
being a soldier for a pair of cavalry boots—yes, for
even a home-made brogan. He would fain have called
upon the pine trees to fall on him and hide him from
those exasperating girls. When he finally escaped and
had gotten to a safe distance he muttered—" Confound

them! I'll bet a thousand dollars they won't catch me in that fix any more." He never went bare-footed again.

The war was now raging in earnest and soon the whole Southland was thrilled with news of the great victory at Manassas. The people went wild with enthusiasm, and while hundreds of families were burdened with sorrow for their loved dead, they rejoiced that those loved ones fell in the hour of triumph. No words can depict the exultation and mad joy of the entire people. Men who had doubted our ability to cope with the North now shouted themselves hoarse in the mighty chorus of victory. Well for the brave boys who perished at Manassas that their young lives went out under a rising sun, while the birds were yet singing and no thought of disaster disturbed the dream of empire. Other battles were fought and other victories were won, but never again were the Confederates to steep their very souls in triumph, for when week after week, and month after month, the armies rushed against each other with stubborn fury, it was found that the people of the North were fighting with a determination that no disaster could appall. When they found that 'ninety days' was a maddening delusion, and "On to Richmond" the death-knell of magnificent armies, they went to work to win, and the world witnessed the most stupendous struggle of modern times, or stood aghast while brothers tore each other's throats with the ferocity of wild beasts.

Joe went off to the army of Tennessee. He had been under fire several times, but his first banquet of blood was on that memorable Sunday morning at Shiloh. How they broke the Federal line of battle; how they stormed battery after battery; how they drove the enemy pell-mell to the bank of the river; how their great leader fell in the hour of victory, and how a halt was called when one more brave rush would have secured the fruits of that day's carnage, are all matters of history. We shall not invade its sacred precincts. The solemn facts of all time are therein recorded, and it deals only with public men or things, while our story tells but the simple lives of two boys who loved each other, and did their duty in an humble way.

When the news came that the Feliciana boys had been in a great battle there was the most intense excitement. The scenes witnessed in the little town of Clinton had a thousand counterparts all over the North and South during four weary years. Loved ones waiting for news of absent loved ones; fathers and mothers anxious about a soldier son; a wife fearfully listening for the truth about her husband; children weeping and wondering on account of their father; the maiden blushing and trembling as she inquires the fate of her gallant lover. God preserve us all from a repetition of such scenes. Once in a lifetime is once too often.

The matter was now coming home to the Feliciana people and they crowded into town to learn the news. Tom went early Tuesday morning anxious to learn the fate of Joe and other young friends who were known to have been in the battle. The telegraph office was upstairs, and some loud-voiced man stood at the window, a living bulletin-board, to let the people hear the messages as they **were ticked off**. The street **was** densely packed with all sorts and conditions of people, all breathless with attention. Suddenly a great silence falls upon the crowd as the party at the window begins to read. Hush! Listen!

"A great battle! Yankee hirelings routed! Immense stores captured or destroyed. Glory and honor to the boys in grey."

Thus on for many minutes was the crowd entertained, and, as one wild statement followed another, men and boys broke into shouts. A hoarse roar of approval swept over the throng, and hurrah followed hurrah, but this was only the orchestral crash before the curtain rose upon the tragedy.

Next came a telegram from Colonel Fisher, giving the details that appealed directly to the hearts of all present. It read as follows:

"Our regiment was closely engaged in the fight both Sunday and Monday, and our boys sustained the proud reputation that Louisianians have already made on the battle-fields of Virginia. They were among the first into the enemy's camp on Sunday morning, and fought with honor all day. During the bloody conflict of Monday they stood like veterans, capturing a battery of three pieces and one stand of colors. I am sorry to report heavy losses both in killed and wounded. We lost twenty-seven men on Sunday and fifty-three during the frightful carnage of the next day. Company A lost its gallant Captain Hargrove, who was shot through the head within twenty yards of the battery and died instantly. [A voice from the crowd, 'God rest his soul, for he was a noble man.'] Sergeant John Holcomb was killed early Sunday, and brave little Willie Manson fell at the head of the regiment bearing its colors."

There was a faint, sad cry heard from the opposite side of the street, and the dead boy's sister Alice was carried fainting away. Name after name was called among the dead until it told of thirteen of the home boys who would never come back. Tom will never forget the fearful fascination of that voice calling the dead-roll of Shiloh. Cry after cry of sorrow and pity arose from the crowd as they heard some well-known name announced among the slain.

Poor Martha Willis had been haunting the telegraph office since dawn, waiting with heavy heart to hear from Robert, and now, when the closing words of the report read: "Robert Willis was mortally wounded, and died Sunday night," she cried in her agony: "Oh, Robert, my darling! They enticed you off to the wars with their fine words about patriotism, and now you are dead. My Robert, dead on the cruel battle-field and your poor wounded face without a coffin! How can I spare you, Robert? Our little home was so bright and happy. Oh, Robert! Robert! my murdered darling!"

In her agony the poor girl forgot that her husband was responsible for his own acts and had joined the army without any compulsion.

Tom heard many sad things that day, and when the reading of the reports was over, climbed down from the horse-rack, where he had taken his stand to see and hear, convinced that war was a terrible thing, and happy that Joe's name was not upon the awful list. Who can ever forget the horrible fascination that draws one to listen to the dead-roll of a battle, especially when a loved one is there whose fate is still uncertain? Tom went home dazed, and yet longing to be with Joe— painfully yearning for the wild revelry of battle. He had no desire to kill anybody, and he never dreamed of being killed. His heart was as tender as a girl's, and no suffering chick or lamed pig but appealed successfully to his warmest sympathies. He would never wantonly shoot one of nature's songsters, and would step aside lest he crushed the worm in his path, but there arose in his bosom a desire to do some startling and heroic thing, such as capturing a gunboat or storming a battery. Of course, he expected to have to hew his way, with a good saber, through crowded columns of Yankees, and doubtless many unfortunate men would perish in his path, yet, without one bloodthirsty thought, they were regarded as necessary obstacles to his ambition which must be removed. Tom was yet at that age when all glory and honor was to be laid at the feet of father and mother, but later on—— yes, later on, we shall see who will come amid the glories and flowers of spring-time, to take the measure of his boyish heart and entangle his soul amid the meshes of her sunny hair. We shall see you tremble with happiness, dear Tom, and we shall feel for you when the waves of sorrow roll over you, wild as the sweep of an ocean tempest.

CHAPTER VIII.

GOODNIGHT.

A FEW years prior to the war, there came into the neighborhood where our boys lived a man whose manner was so different from the ways of that people that he became at once an object of interest, and of no little curiosity. Of gigantic form, and carrying, or rather being carried, by what old Uncle Zeb called "de most ongodliest pair o' foots," he was a source of endless amusement to the boys—of ridicule, also, until they learned to know him. His face was a true index to his character—honest and kindly, strong and determined, yet lacking the polish of the higher social and intellectual life, and his dress was not after any style that was ever seen in the drawing-room. No one could ever imagine him dressed otherwise than in copperas breeches and a coat of dirty brown. If he ever wore a white shirt he kept the fact a profound secret. It must not be supposed that he was slovenly in his dress, or lacked neatness in his person. On the contrary, his clothing was kept clean, although it might offend the esthetic eye, and his hair, while long, after the fashion of those days, was never unkempt. Clothes do not make the man, but there are some styles of clothing and men that are inseparable.

This man came afoot into Louisiana, carrying a little bundle, and upon his shoulder a very long small-bore rifle. He had some money with him, but there had been small occasion to use it, for in those days a man could travel, on foot or horseback, from Texas to Maryland at no expense for living, nor was he regarded a tramp, and expected to chop stove-wood for his breakfast. The old-time hospitality of the South was such that a man who made a traveler pay for a night's lodging was considered stingy. They had not then learned to call it thrift, and to refuse to entertain the stranger was regarded a small meanness. It would be a little hazardous now to attempt such a trip without money, and the tramp is in constant danger of a conflict with dogs.

When Caleb Knight, in his wanderings, reached the old Jefford place, one of the earliest settlements, which for some cause had been abandoned, he found there a small house of two rooms, which, being quite habitable, seemed to suit his fancy, and without any ceremony he took possession. Being expert with tools, which he was able to borrow from the carpenter of a neighboring plantation, he soon made such repairs as were necessary, and rigged up such articles of furniture as were requisite to his modest wants. With the judicious expenditure of a little money, he procured a supply of such things as he could not make, getting them hauled out from town by a kindly darkey who was returning with an empty wagon.

In that quiet neighborhood the advent of a stranger was a matter of considerable speculation, and, as we have stated, the neighbors became very much interested in this man ; for no such specimen could be found from "Possum Corner," in the northwest, to "Pig Trot," in the extreme southeastern portion of the parish. After the manner of the old Bible stories speculation begat rumor, rumor begat suspicion, and suspicion begat report, until it was generally supposed that this man Caleb was a bloody Abolitionist in disguise, for whom a rope with the hangman's knot was the proper thing. The question became a burning one, for if he were allowed to remain who knew but they would all "wake up some morning and find themselves dead ;" so it came about, as a result of these wild rumors, that within ten days after this stranger had settled himself he was waited upon by a committee of citizens to inquire into his business and intentions. This committee had been selected at an informal meeting held under the great beech tree in front of the country church, while the good people were waiting for the preaching hour to arrive, and was composed of Colonel DuPree, Judge Mabry, and Major Carter—a very dignified and imposing trio, we may well imagine, and well calculated to make any evil-doer tremble in his shoes, no matter how large.

Bright and early on Monday morning those gentlemen met as agreed at the cross-roads and proceeded on their errand of investigation. They felt fully as important as does the average "Congressional committee" when venturing now-a-days into the untamed South in search of political outrages, and probably suffered equal trepidation, but they went forward bravely and soon found Caleb seated under the wide-spreading branches of a mighty oak near his cottage, very busily engaged in making a cane fish-trap. Now these traps are quite simple in their construction, yet requiring some skill to make properly, and when carefully placed in the creek rarely fail to reward the owner, or some poacher, with a mess of perch or suckers. They are formed of the long reed canes that grow near the water, are cylindrical in shape, being fastened around oak or hickory hoops with some stringy bark for wrapping twine, and one end is left open with a funnel-shaped throat through which the fish enter. This throat is so arranged that the fish can pass in readily, but in trying to return they find it easier to pass by the opening than go through it.

Riding up to the spot where the trap-builder was seated, Judge Mabry, who was spokesman for the party, opened the momentous discussion by saying : "Good morning, Mr. Knight." Very pleasantly Caleb responded to this tremendous salutation :

"Same to you all, gentulmen. Git down and let your tackies rest, an' we'll git a'quainted. Powerful warm for so soon in the season, an' I reckon this summer's gwinter be a regler scorcher in this hot climit."

The committee, seeing that their man was not slow to talk, dismounted, and found comfortable seats in the shade.

"Well, gentulmen, I'm powerful glad to see you. Here I've been for two weeks an' not a white man have

I seed except now an' then one passing along the big
road. I like good, quiet kind of people who 'tends to
their own business, and I like to live away out here in
the kuntry. Lawd help me, but I wouldn't live in
town for no inducements. Why, sir, I went down to
Wilmington away yonder last summer an' I aint hardly
got over it yet, sech a rattle of kyarts an' tootin of whis-
sels was enuf to give a man the bline-staggers. Unly
stayed there two days when I lit out fer the mountins
whar I camped an' hunted fer three weeks, jest to steddy
my nerves like. Did either of you men ever go to
Wilmington? No! Well, gentulmen, that is a town
fer you. Sech a rale tare-up and smash-out noise, an'
hubbub, and hooraw you never heard, ceppen you've
been through a saw-mill in full tilt, knocken nots an
winshakes right an' left. Give me the kuntry every
time, an' I'll live or die'a-tryin'."

It looked like the interviewers had caught a hungry
parrot, until in one lucky moment Caleb paused a little
to turn his trap and insert a fresh piece of bark-warp,
when Judge Mabry rushed to the charge:

"We came over this morning, Mr. Knight, to get
acquainted with you and find out something about you.
These are troublous times and many suspicious strangers are roaming through the country—some as ped-
dlers, and some in the guise of book-agents. We wish
to locate you properly, and if you are all right we will
make it very pleasant for you"—"An' ef I aint all right,
you are gwinter make it hot fer me I reckon," interposed Caleb.

"Oh, no doubt you are all right," resumed the Judge; "but I should judge from your remarks about Wilmington that you are from that section of the country—possibly from Pennsylvania."

"Whar's that you say I'm frum? Pen-Pen-Pensyl-vany? Why, doggone my skin, that's a Yankee State, an' you mean to let on that I'm a Yankee, do you? Well, I kin jess nacherly wallop the hindsights off of any three men in this ole allegater State what sez I'm frum any sech a kuntry. I'm from the free State of ole North Carliney, I am, an' I dont keer who knows it. I wus born only about twenty steps frum the blessed old French Broad river, an' I lived for thirty years whar I could be in a swimmin one minit an' the next minit could clime up nearer to Heaven than any of you will ever git. I'm a regler tar-heel, I am, an' hevn't hed my hans free from rossum a week at a time, fer twenty years. If ever I go back on the ole State I hope that some bigger man than I am will up an' call me a Yankee peddler."

Caleb was very touchy on the subject of his nativity, and had that native Southern antipathy to the name "Yankee." In fact, for many years it was a term of reproach that was a deadly insult when applied to one born South, and must be atoned for. The giant's wrath was aroused, and, rising to his feet, he doubled his mighty fists like two great hams, and assuming an attitude of defiance, invited the committee to "wade right in an' git mashed." His usually passive face was lighted with pugilistic fires, and his immense fect were planted upon the earth with the power of Enceladus.

Our titled gentlemen were all alarmed at these warlike demonstrations, and hastened to disclaim any intentional offense. They also very promptly declined the invitation to "wade in," and Colonel DuPree interposed with:

"Why, friend Knight, you certainly misunderstood the Judge. He was not trying to make game of you or your State. There are two Wilmingtons—one in Delaware and the other in North Carolina. Of course, the Delaware town doesn't begin to compare with your North Carolina city—should not be mentioned during the same day—but it's a rattling good town, and a man needn't be ashamed to say he lived there. You may rest easy on the Yankee question, my good man, for no one with a half an eye would ever charge you with such nativity. We are your friends, Mr. Knight, and you may depend upon us."

"Well, ser," replied Caleb, "I know'd it was agin reason for sech pleasant-faced gentlemen as you all 'pear to be to poke fun at a poor fellow like me, much less layin' sech charges agin me as bein' a Yankee, but when you sed I wus from that outlandish country with the long name I was riled all of a sudden. I'm from old North Carliney, I am, an' I don't keer who knows it."

"We are very glad, Mr. Knight, to know that you are from the noble old State of North Carolina, the very home of freedom and the American eagle," replied the Judge. "I am from South Carolina, myself, and

am proud to acknowledge it. I had the honor to be
present on that memorable occasion when the famous
remark was made about the length of time between
drinks. The Governors of both States were present, but
I am not certain which one was father to that historic
remark ; it is enough to know that the time didn't grow
any longer. I never drink, and did not personally
applaud the sentiment, but most of those present considered that discussion the very essence of eloquence."

Caleb looked at the Judge with an incredulous smile
upon his honest face and remarked :

"Law, law, Jedge—if you could jest take one fair
swig of the mountin dew we fabricates up in the hills
of ole North Carliney, you never would draw another
sober breath while you live—exceppen you wus a mighty
strong 'terminated man."

The party had settled down again on friendly terms
but the committeemen were at a loss how to proceed.
They could not see their way to any further investigation of Caleb's history without the risk of another
explosion, and in fact his blunt ways with quaint hon-
esty of expression had impressed them favorably. They
realized the fact that they had stumbled upon a character different from anything they had known. They
remained seated in the shade, and Major Carter com-
mented upon the build and usefulness of fish-traps.
He told how his son Bob had brought in as fine a mess
of goggle-eyed perch and blue-cat, "one morning last
week" as he had ever seen, and Colonel DuPree discussed the prospects of the cotton crop. He declared

that the young plant was "growing so rapidly these recent warm days" that he should put a dozen hands to chopping out the blue-gum field the next morning. Judge Mabry said that his son Joe had killed a wild gobbler with a beard ten inches long, on the last Saturday morning, and that the great bird was so fat it furnished its own grease in cooking. When the committee had all spoken they seemed to be at their wit's end. A good alligator story or a twenty-one rattled rattlesnake would have been a godsend to the party, but the spirit of anecdote would not come at their call, and conversation began to fail.

About this time Caleb finished wrapping the trap and came to their relief by suddenly springing the question which had brought him these unexpected visitors. He said:

"I calkerlate, gentulmen, that I can guess what brought you all here to-day, and I'm gwinter tell you what you wanter know, so as to save your feelins. You wanter find out whar I come from an' about what I'm gwinter do. Well, I've told you I'm from ole North Carliney, an' I don't keer who knows it. Jist why I am here is what you don't know, an' hev been too perlite to ax me, but if you all will promise me not to talk it 'round I'll tell you what made me skin out from ole North Carliney and live here in a style unbecomin enny white man. Shore nuff now, gentulmen, will you keep my story?"

The committee agreed, and assured him that any statement he might make would be kept inviolate.

"Very well, then, gentulmen, make yourselves easy on that log an' I'll tell you how come you see me here. I don't look like a man what would have enny luv trubbles, do I, Kernel?"

"Why," responded the astonished Colonel, "I am sure I don't see why you shouldn't fall in love as well as any one else. You are not more than thirty years old, and any man of your age is liable to the tender passion if he meets a charming girl. I have known more unlikely cases than yours—old white-headed men sometimes make fools of themselves about women. You are big enough to fall in love."

"Now you're shoutin', ole hoss! (beg your pardon,) an' enny man expressin' sech sound doctrine as that will do to go on a camp hunt. You are my friend, Kernel, an' you, Jedge, an' you, Major, an' I'm your'n to count on in enny part of the mountins." Here he gave each one of his visitors a tremendous grip of the hand and continued :

" As I was gwinter say, I'm from old North Carliney, an' I don't keer who knows it. I left there kinder onexpected like, all on account of old man Warner's gal, Susan, but she was the notablest gal in all that kuntry for forty miles, up and down the French Broad, an' you know, gentulmen, that is the purtiest river that ever run down hill.

"Ole man Warner—that's Susan's daddy—kep the boss still of the mountins, I tell you, an' it wus shore-nuf whisky, without enny 'dulterations, also, gen-tul-men, she was a shore-nuf gal, without enny make-up.

Well, ser, I kep comp'ny with Susan right peart all
last summer, an' on until tobacco-curing time, an' it
'peared to me that I wus jest as good as son-in-law to
the old man, but you caint always tell. Gals is awful
oncertain, an' there's no knowin' when you've got 'em.
Sometimes, even when the preacher has tied the knot,
an' you are shore you've got 'em, it turns out that
they've got you instead. One night, along in October,
there wus a big party over on the creek about ten
miles, at Jim Whalley's, an' if you'll b'leeve me, gen-
telmen, that gal never let me tech her. Whenever I
cum nigh her she wus that skittish an' scornful-like I
jest went away an' left her, but she danced seven sets
with a red-complected feller named Pete Brownlow, an'
the way she smiled on him wus plum agrivatin'. She
would look so pleased whenever he cum about her it
made me mad, an' I dubbled up my fists untel they
hed the cramps. Oh! I tell you I wus howlin' mad,
an' about midnight I went home, but I never slep' a
wink. I walked about the yard for a hour or two, an'
then I climed away up onto a big rock on the mount'in
side, where I looked fust up to the stars away yonder
in the hevens, a-shinin' an' a-glitterin', then I looked
down into the river, where it sloshed an' tumbled over
the rock. The stars wus a-shinin' and a-glitterin'
down there. Gentulmen, I hed murder in my heart
when I clim'ed up onto that rock, for I know'd that
Pete Brownlow had been liein' to Susan about me, but
after awhile the world seemed so still that my wrath
settled down. The ugly spirit left me, an' I felt as cam

as if there warn't a gal in the whole universe of God.
Kernel, I don't see how any man can go out under the
stars at night an' keep ugly things in his heart—they
seem to me like a thousand eyes looking me right
through and through.

"Next day I met Pete 'gwine up the road toward ole
man Warner's house, an gentulmen, the devil wus in
me biggern a mule in less time 'n 'twould take you to
say ' *scat.*'   I stopt him right in the road an told him
he hed been licin' to Susan about me, an' I wus gwinter
wallop the very gizzard outen him.   He was a spunky
fellow an' 'sputed it.   He low'd I wus only jellus because
Susan perferred a decent sized man like him to a great
overgrown he-bar like me, an' he sed no likely young
gal like Susan could luv a man what wore number
fourteen boots.   I know I've got a big foot, but, Kernel,
do you think that ought to be ennything agin a man
in a gal's affections?"

"By no means," responded the Colonel; "you are
a very large man and a small foot would not serve
your purposes, besides, only silly girls and sillier boys
worry about large feet."

"Well, gentulmen," resumed Caleb, "the devil in me
got bigger an' bigger untel I coulder mashed Pete right
then an' thar, so I told him to prepare his feelens for the
durndest whoopin that enny red-headed man ever got.
He wern't afraid, not one bit, but he low'd I wus too big
for him an' he wouldn't hev no fair showin' in a rough-
and-tumble rukus, so I told him jest to tie my right-
hand behine my back an' let the row begin. Gentulmen,

you bet he tied it tite, an' then before you could say
'*scat*' two times he waltzed around in front of me an'
hit me sech a dip in the stumuck that I couldn't hear
it thunder for about two minits. You better believe
me he wus a wiry fellow, an' that active that I had
most as well try to hit a weasel. The way he danced
around me an' hit me wus a caution to fools, an' I begin
to think that maby I hed made a fool of myself shore-
nuf in hitchin up my best arm, but bimeby I got a
chance to soc him one with my left-fist, an' 'ser, he went
to grass. Did you ever see a big fox-squirrel drap
when my ole rifle speaks-out? Gentulmen, the devil
wus in me awful big when I hit Pete that lick, but
when he tumbled over the bluff that skirts that mountin road, an' I heard him roll down shakin' the bushes
an' rattlin the rocks as he went, if you bleeve me, the
old devil was gone in a minit! I believe you kin skeer
the devil outen a man quickern you kin preach him out,
an' when you take fire an' brimstone outen the hereafter you lose your grip on many a likely young church
member."

This doctrine of Caleb's is yet orthodox with most
of the churches, but many of the ministry are hiding it away on a shelf alongside that awful dogma
of "infant damnation." May we not in getting rid
of a future hell run the risk of finding it in this
life?

"When the noise of Pete's fallin' hushed," said Caleb,
"I felt that faint and sick-like about the stumuck—
worsen when he hit me that fust lick, but I run round

to a little cow-path down the hill an' away down towards the bottom I found him layin there pale-lookin and still. I pulled him the best I could with my one hand into a more cumferbler position, then I brought sum water in my hat frum the creek an' poured on his face, but he wouldn't cum to. I did feel so bad about it, though I knowd I didn't mean to kill him shore nuf. I hit him like I wus gwinter bust him plum open because I wus mad, but now I wus awful sorry; so after a while when I could see there wus life in him still, I felt easier an' concluded to git some help.

"I lit out up the road towards ole man Warner's, which was the nighest house, an' on the way I met little Si Owens—he wus a sort of a half-fool of a boy an' didn't have no sense—an' I got him to cut the string that helt my right hand so I wouldn't appear so redickerlus in case I met any sensible peepul. If you bleeve me the little fool laffed an' laffed untel I felt like slappin the seven senses outen him, but I didn't do it, an' went on untel I struck the Warner gate. The first purson I seed wus Susan a settin on the piazzer doin sum sorter soin. She made like she didn't see me an' you bet that riled me, so I up an' told her that if she would go down there jest under the bluff she would find her luvey-duvey, Peetsy-weetsy, a layin there with his whole frame onjinted. You see the devil wus a gitten back into me his full size, an' wus rather crowdin me, so I didn't keer much what I sed. I noticed she turned fust mighty red an' then mighty white, an' then she got red agin shore nuf. A rale mad woman gits mighty red in the face an' don't always look purty as she oughter.

"Susan fired up tremenjously an' told me I wus a fool. I knowed that much already, so I warn't alarmed, but when she told me to take my big feet away from there, or let' em carry me off, 'fore she turned ole Bulger loose, I got mad. Gentulmen, that Bulger wus a awful dog an' I concluded to go, but as I backed off from the gate I told her she had better go down with sum help to Pete, an' if she found him alive, which warn't likely, tell him to be forever keerful how he run agin the fist of a left-handed man.

"I aint seed Susan since, an' I reckon I never will see her enny more, but, gentulmen, she wus a likely young woman. I made strate home from thar, got my rifle, a few close, and what little money I had, and struck out towards the settin' sun. You bleeve me, I've walked over a power of country since last October, untel now I am settled down here, whar I mean to stay if my nabors will let me.

"Now, sers, you know about all I can tell you, an' if you aint satisfied I'll jog on."

There were tears in the poor fellow's eyes when he finished his story, to which the committee had listened with unflagging interest. No one seeing his honest face and hearing his straightforward way of telling what causes led to his present location could doubt his truth, and when our friends rode away they agreed that there was no harm in him, and that with a little encouragement he might become quite a useful citizen.

4

Thus it came about that our man was left to dwell in peace, and many little useful articles were added to his comfort. The Judge gave him a cow and calf, and Colonel DuPree offered him a pony to ride, but Caleb thanked him, saying he could get over more ground in one day than any pony outside of old "North Carliney."

"Ef I wus to try to ride that critter," he mused, "when I straightened out my legs it would walk right out from under me, an' if I should ride it one hour I'd hev to tote it the next, so I better let it alone."

He soon became a great favorite with the grown-up boys of the neighborhood and many were the hunting and fishing frolics he took with them; but for a camp hunt Caleb was a "whole team," and could furnish more genuine amusement around the fire at night than a whole corps of minstrels. He could sing the queerest songs and tell the funniest stories that the boys had ever heard, nor could anybody equal him in undressing the game and preparing choice bits for supper.

If the boys were fond of Caleb he was no less fond of them, and our Joe seemed to be his especial favorite. It was amusing to observe the intimacy between the bright boy of fifteen and this great double-sized man. The contrast was not greater between David and Mr. Micawber, but two years later when Joe donned the gray uniform he had attained the stature of a man, and people who knew the sterling merit of each ceased to wonder at the strange companionship. While Caleb was really poor as regarded property and education, so great was his moral worth, so uncompromising his integrity, and so utterly was he devoid of sycophancy, or any species of servility, that his companionable presence was always welcome in the proudest homes of the neighborhood. His uncouth language was pardoned because of the excellent sense he always displayed in conversation. The girls all adored him, in a friendly way, and never made fun of him. The boys counted on him always.

He had some peculiar notions about the negro which would hardly have been tolerated in another person. One day Colonel DuPree offered him the position of overseer, or manager, of his immense plantation at a good salary, but the great-hearted fellow declined, and gave his reasons thus:

"I am obleeged to you, Kernel, for the offer, but I caint accept. I aint the right sort of man, an' couldn't do you no good. I never wus used to niggers nohow, for in the mountins of ole North Carliney they wus skaser than pianners, an' I don't know much about 'em. Then there's another thing—I have hyearn that to keep a nigger strate you've got to whup him. I aint no doubt in my mind from what I've seed of the nigger that he needs a heap of whupin, but I never could have the heart to whup a purson who dasent fite back. I don't mind wolloping a mean white man, nor a mean nigger nuther if so be he specially needs it, but he must have a fightin chance."

Caleb had unwittingly told the story—how shameful it was to whip a poor wretch who could not fight back.

CHAPTER IX.

HOW THE OLD HOME DISAPPEARED.

AT the battle of Shiloh our Joe was conspicuous for his gallantry. Not that he was braver than thousands of heroic men on that tremendous day, but when his regiment was wavering under a wasting fire of grape and canister he caught up the standard from the dying hand of little Willie Manson, and stopping but for a word of cheer to the noble boy, rushed to the head of the column and encouraged the suffering troop to more desperate efforts. For this act he was promised promotion, but it never came until upon many a bloody field he had established fully his right to advancement.

Events now crowded one upon another with fierce earnestness until during the hot summer of 1863 we find Joe with his regiment where Johnston fronted Grant at Mississippi's capital. He was getting to be an old soldier now, at the mature age of nineteen, and had seen enough of horrors to make him old in feeling as well.

By some strange fate our young soldier's regiment was in line in the yard and orchard of the old home, and on the same ground where his boyhood had witnessed many a mimic battle of boys, Joe was now to take part in the death struggle of men.

(76)

One bright morning the enemy massed a powerful force on the edge of the wood beyond the orchard—the same wood where Joe and Tom used to gather hickory-nuts or chinquapins in the autumn, and wild jessamines, with violets, in the spring time—and under cover of a tremendous artillery fire prepared to assault the Confederate lines. Battery after battery joined in the mighty duel, and as the heavy sound went booming down the Pearl valley the timid deer sought a deeper covert and the hungry saurian bellowed his defiance. Soon the sharp rattle of musketry in front told that the advance was hard at it. Joe was near the old well-house in the yard waiting with anxious determination for the bloody work so rapidly approaching, when *scher-r-r-r*, crash! and a twelve-pound shell broke through the wall of the mansion and exploded in the little corner room where our boys used to sleep, knocking it into ruins and shaking the house from roof to cellar. Again and again the iron destruction burst through the walls until the dear old home was a pitiful ruin; then as the flames joined in the work of demolition Joe brushed away his tears, and grasping his musket firmly, turned away to meet the coming foe. Back with a rush came the skirmishers, followed by the shouting enemy, and as they reached the shelter of their own lines the battle joined in earnest. A perfect flame of fire swept out from the Confederate front, piling the Federals in scores along the edge of the orchard and for a moment checking their advance—but only for a moment, when several brave officers rushed to the front, sword in hand, and encouraging the men by word or example, the entire body, save the dead and dying, swept grandly forward. But they rushed only to destruction as those terrible volleys successively broke their ranks, and ere they could reform the Confederates were upon them with the bayonet, completing the ruin of that splendid column which emerged from the woods so gallantly a few minutes before.

Thus did Joe see the last of the old home, and thus did he help avenge its destruction. He bore himself with more than usual courage that morning and never knew how proud his homefolks were when they read in the report of the battle: "Sergeant Joseph Mabry, for conspicuous gallantry in capturing a stand of colors, is recommended for promotion"—nor was his modest demeanor changed when he assumed the duties of first lieutenant.

Jennie read the report in her far-away home and wondered if her woman's judgment had not erred in ascribing Joe's conduct in the valentine party episode to a lack of courage, instead of a courage more sublime than that age could appreciate.

The wave of war had brought Joe back to within one hundred and fifty miles of Belhaven, but bore him as swiftly away; then came more long marches, and heroic fighting, until two months later we find him still clinging to his musket all through two dreadful days at Chickamauga. Here he did his duty with all the headlong valor of his ancestor who rode with

Marion one hundred years ago. Overwhelming victory remained with the Confederates, but the fearful loss of life was a blow they felt unto the end. Such determined courage was never surpassed on any field, and the soldiers of both armies had no reason to be ashamed of their prowess. It was a rare thing in those old days for either army to find out the exact time when it was whipped, and a great battle was generally a series of charges and counter charges, of flight and pursuit for a mile or more, then the pursuer in turn put to flight and followed back over the same ground. These things generally lasted a day or two, and occasionally for several days, when the two armies would settle down for a few weeks while the pickets would pop away at each other, or swap coffee for tobacco.

Joe had been in many battles, and, while sometimes meeting with reverses, the army had suffered no total defeat, but the day was rapidly approaching when it was to be overwhelmed and driven from its chosen position in front of Chattanooga by the veterans of Thomas and Grant. Never, in all the annals of the war, were the Confederates so completely routed, and that, too, when they were exulting in the hope that they were about to complete the work so bravely begun at Chickamauga. The Army of Tennessee had now to cope with their old enemy whom they had whipped at Shiloh, but who came in front of them here with the proud new title, "Conqueror of Vicksburg." There was a fearful conflict at Missionary Ridge, but the Confederates fought as soldiers always fight when they find themselves outgeneraled. Military criticism is unavailing. We must accept the verdict of history and acknowledge a crushing defeat where we had been looking for an overwhelming triumph.

Joe's regiment held its ground until bayonets were clashing in front, and a blue column was sweeping around on the flank; then came the supreme moment when a soldier must determine to die at his post, or take such action as will enable him to—

" Live to fight another day."

It is very easy to talk about dying heroically in front of battle, thereby gaining much immediate praise and straightway be forgotten, but to the average man it seems quite uncomfortable and foolish—especially is this so when no personal or public good can be accomplished by martyrdom. Robert Lee and his worn-out veterans retreating to Appomattox form the sublimest picture of any age.

To be a hero does not necessarily imply that a soldier should never show his back to the foe. Sometimes it is very prudent and eminently proper to do so, and, in these days of long-range rifles, you want to make the display at a great distance. The day for dying merely to prove your courage is past—it sometimes requires more courage to live.

Joe fought as he always did, even when a school-boy, with his whole soul put into his work. When the Confederate line was broken he clubbed his musket, and, whirling it about him with tremendous fury, knocked aside more than one advancing bayonet. Slowly he gave back before the advancing foe; the stock of his musket was soon broken, and upon one knee trying to parry the thrust of a half score of bayonets, he thought that for him the supreme moment had indeed arrived. Can nothing save him? Must the brave boy perish in the hour of defeat?

Even as a gallant Federal officer sprang to protect him from the steel of the soldiers, there came a ringing crash as when a mighty hammer strikes the anvil and shattered muskets are hurled to the earth. The blue line is for a moment broken, a strong hand grasps Joe's arm, and a familiar voice shouts in his ear: "Let's git away from here, Joe!" The stroke that parried the vengeful bayonets was from the powerful arm of Caleb Knight, wielding the barrel of a broken rifle, and the friendly voice was his. Then was seen some "tall running" as Joe and Caleb sped down that fatal hillside and joined their comrades in a sullen stand that checked the career of the victors, and inspired with new courage the defeated army of Bragg. Without the timely help of Caleb our Joe would have been killed, or taken prisoner, but let us see how the giant North Carolinian came so opportunely.

We have shown how in hunting and fishing frolics Caleb had become much attached to our young soldier, and when Joe joined Captain Hargrove's company, he was present but could not be induced to become a member. He had his own peculiar notions about the war, and some of them were shared by a large proportion of the non-slaveholding element of the South. Many persons, like Judge Mabry, opposed secession, but yielded to the force of events and gave their allegiance to the State, and finally to the Confederacy. Others considered the claims of the Union stronger than the rights of the individual States, and many of these found it extremely uncomfortable to remain in the South—justly so, too, in most instances. There were yet other thousands who entered the Federal army and fought against their old-time neighbors. It was the old story of a house divided and not able to stand.

Caleb often visited at Judge Mabry's, and feeling himself welcome would drop in at any time, bringing a string of fish or a bag of squirrels, and occasionally an old king gobbler whose beard trailed the ground. On account of his excellent qualities the boys called him "Goodnight"—a name bestowed upon him by Joe, and which stuck to him ever afterwards. He rather liked the name, so we shall try to remember the fact as we go on. After Joe went off to the army, he used to come over to the Judge's quite often to make inquiries, and would always have some pleasant word to send.

One afternoon near the end of May, when all the family were seated on the front gallery discussing events and speculating on the future, the Judge asked Goodnight to tell him why he opposed the war and would not become a soldier?

"Well, Jedge," responded the giant, "I ain't seed no occasion for it yet. The United States is gooder nuf

fer me." "That's just what I said at first," interposed
Tom, "but I'm converted now, and I'll bet a thousand
dollars you are a rebel in less than a month."

"Tom, I seed a fox-squirrel in that big hickory down
at the corner as I cum up the road. Hadn't you better
go shoot it?" Then Goodnight resumed his statement:
"Ole North Carliney wus the first to start the family a
long time ago, so I don't yit feel no call to break up
the arrangement. I like to know what I'm fiten about
and then I kin peel off my coat and wade rite in fer
who last the longest. We poor folks think it's all a
rich man's war, an' onless we seed the good reason fer
it, we don't take no stock in it. I spose if we had lots
of niggers, like Kernel DuPree, an' tothers who are
gitten the row a goin, we mout look at it differnt, but
we ain't got the niggers, and we ain't gwinter fite fer
'em. Didn't you never notice, Jedge, that most people
think like it pays 'em to think?"

"Look here, Goodnight," responded the Judge, "if
the Yankees send down their soldiers and undertake
to destroy our property, or take away our liberties,
what are you going to do? You know I was a Union man,
and am one still if matters can be arranged, but if we are
invaded—and such seems to be the case in Virginia—
I am for fight, no matter how much I love our common
country. Now, sir, what are you going to do? You
must take one side or the other, for there will be no
neutral position in this war."

"Well, now, Jedge, you looker here yourself. You
are a pinin' me down mighty close, an' you are a ser-

posin' things, but, gentulmen, if the wust comes to the wust I'm gwinter fite uv course, an' I'll jest bump the head of the first Yankee I find, be he peddler or soldier. Ole North Carliney aint't serceded yit, an' I'm gwinter wait to see what she'll do, but you may load it into your rifle an' shoot it into a tree, that ef ole North Carliney sercedes, I'll sercede too."

A burst of applause from the family followed this last speech, and Tom, turning a half dozen hand-springs on the front walk, cried: "Hurrah for old Goodnight! The Yankees might as well give up. Won't we make them skeedaddle? Goodnight, you are a regular whizzer!"

"What is a whizzer, Tom?" asked his mother.

"A whizzer, mother? Oh, pshaw! A whizzer is a —— is a —— a whizzer is a fellow who makes things whiz,"—then the Judge told Tom he thought that would be sufficient for one afternoon and he had better go for the cows.

In the course of a few weeks the pressure of events was so great that North Carolina did "sercede," and as soon as he heard the news Goodnight came over and told the Judge that he had "serceded, too," and was going off to join the army and take care of Joe. He put in an appearance at regimental headquarters while the army was resting near Corinth, and told Colonel Fisher that he wanted to be with the Feliciana boys and take a hand in any fighting that might occur; but he declined to submit to regular duty as a soldier. He said he wanted to "skrimmage around" on his own responsibility, and that if any Yankee fooled with him somebody would get hurt. The Colonel informed him that it would be necessary for him to be regularly enrolled in the service if he desired to be treated as a prisoner of war in the event of his capture by the enemy, and also if he wished to draw rations or pay. This was rather a mountain in his way, but when the boys of Captain Hargrove's company, including his friend Joe Mabry, testified to Goodnight's excellent character and his marvelous skill with the rifle, it was arranged that he should become a member of that company, but have a roving commission as scout with permission to come and go as he pleased. This suited him exactly, and he made himself very much at home about Joe's mess where he was always welcome. One of the few long range rifles in the Confederate service was secured for him, and he promised to "make it airn its feed," nor have we any reason to doubt that he kept his promise. At Shiloh he was in the skirmish line; at Murfreesboro he brought in a couple of prisoners; at Chickamauga he was complimented for bringing down a gallant Federal field officer at nearly eight hundred yards, and now at Missionary Ridge we find him with a broken rifle bringing up the rear of the Confederate army, and lamenting that his pet weapon was forever ruined. The spoils of war from many a bloody field enabled the authorities to readily replace the lost gun with a better, and Goodnight was off as a scout once more.

General Grant was not the man to neglect following up an advantage. He put everything in order, and

then leaving his able lieutenant to press the mighty
struggle with Johnston, who had succeeded Bragg, he
flew to Virginia to match arms with that incomparable
leader, the heroic Robert E. Lee. Thither our story
shall follow him—or rather meet him, for it seemed to
be the fortune of our young soldier to cope in an humble way with one of the foremost warriors of modern
times.

In the latter part of April, 1864, Lieutenant Joseph
Mabry, through the influence of Colonel DuPree, who
now held an important position in the War Department
at Richmond, was transferred to the Army of Northern
Virginia. It was hard for Joe to leave his old comrades, but most of the boys with whom he had been
intimate had perished on the field, or were fretting
away their lives in prison, so there were but few to
leave. Our worthy scout obtained leave to go with
Joe, and together they reported for duty just as the
last tremendous thunders of the Wilderness were tolling the requiem of twenty thousand dead Americans.
In the latter days of the war the soldiers were not con-
sulted as to their choice of officers, and Joe was as-
signed to duty as lieutenant in a Georgia regiment.
He soon won the regard of his men by his considerate
manner and never-failing courage. Amid the awful
carnage of Spotsylvania he endeared himself to those
brave fellows forever, and, upon the death of its captain,
succeeded to the command of the company.

It is not our province to record that gigantic struggle from the Wilderness to Petersburg; how the great

combatants writhed back and forth in the grapple of death until the blood of seventy thousand heroes watered the hills and valleys around Richmond, but it is enough that we follow our Joe through those dreadful weeks and months, when ten thousand fell at his right hand, and the darts of the grim Terror showered about him like hailstones from a summer cloud. He went about his duties with no rest from marching and fighting, but amid all those scenes of blood his tender heart never hardened and his lofty purpose never weakened.

Goodnight was ever on the scout, and so careful was his investigation, so sound his conclusions, that General Lee often sent the brave fellow to bring him certain news of the movements of some column of the enemy. He was often at the tent of the commander, but he always felt that he was in a superior presence, and would lift his hat while yet twenty yards away. No danger could appal our scout, and his simple heart felt no dictates save those of stern, unflinching duty. He aimed his deadly rifle with no desire for blood, but simply as a matter of patriotic duty, and always with a mental prayer that his enemy might "die easy."

CHAPTER X.

CHRISTMAS, 1864.

GENERAL LEE made his last tremendous struggle for the dying Confederacy during nine eventful months in front of Petersburg, and there day after day his gallant soldiers perished around him. With an endurance both heroic and pathetic they bared their breasts to an overwhelming enemy, and grew haggard under the insidious approaches of another enemy more powerful than the legions of Grant; they slowly starved as they fought. For weeks at a time there was the most desperate struggle as the Federal leader vainly tried to break the line of defence; then would come a season of comparative repose, disturbed only by the crash of shells and the annoying *zip* of the sharp-shooters' bullet.

Joe was a captain now and no longer carried a musket. So thorough was he in discipline and so ever ready for duty that he attracted the attention of his general, and the youthful officer found his soldier life more pleasant than at any time since the war began. On the horrible 30th of July, 1864, it was Joe's company that led the friendly succor rushing to the help of the torn and mangled regiment that had endured the fires of hell at the "Crater." The exigences of war will excuse many things that are shocking to the civilian mind, but never the murder of sleeping men, and modern warfare records nothing more inhuman than the dreadful slaughter of those South Carolina troops on the breastworks in front of Petersburg. The British justified the blowing of Sepoys from the cannon mouth by pointing to their awful crimes, and this was after trial; but humanity revolts when brave men, whose only offense is heroic defense of rights and property, are allowed no chance for their lives. The act was barbarous, and will forever cast a shadow over an illustrious fame, but the retribution which the God of battles sometimes thunders upon the evil-doer came swift and terrible. The call of blood crying from the ground for vengeance was never more fully answered than when a few hours later four thousand Federal dead were piled in one sickening mass amid the ruins of the mighty explosion. Confusion suddenly darkened their counsels, and shameful defeat marked a day they hoped to make forever famous. Just inside the lines, where a monument now marks the wreck of a Massachusetts regiment, Joe's column struck the enemy with indescribable fury and checked their triumphant progress. The Federals fought that day like men who had no heart and their opponents with the blind fury of tigers. When the blue column reached the scene of the explosion and saw men dying with horrible burns; some poor wretches begging to be pulled from under the wreck, and others calling piteously for water, those soldiers whose bravery had won triumph after triumph for their cause were conquered in the presence of their own sickening work. They fought not with their old-time alacrity, but as men who were ashamed of the ruin they had wrought.

For meritorious conduct at the "mine explosion" our Joe was the next day promoted to the rank of major.

"I'm with you, Joe," cried Goodnight, as they hurried to the battle, and his faithful rifle spoke out clear amid the rattle of many muskets. The smoke of awful conflict settled down over the scene, and when it arose the two armies were back in their original positions. The largest grave ever hollowed by human means was filled with victims, and the bitter hatred which yet rankles in thousands of hearts took on another degree of bitterness.

That evening when Goodnight came to report his day's work to Joe (his invariable custom) he patted his rifle affectionately as he said:

"She airned her feed to-day, Joe. I fired down on them niggers and white men in that great big hole until I'm plum sick. The Lord forgive me, but I bleeve I'm gitten blood-thirsty an' ain't satisfied onless I'm shootin' at some poor Yankee. There I wus a shootin' them fellers in that hole with a warm feelin' inside of me like I wus eatin' a good dinner. Joe, I do hate to shoot at men who don't hev no fair chance to shoot back, but they dug the hole an' got in it, so what wus I to do? Ef this thing would jest stop I would give my chance of ever seein' ole North Carliney agin."

But the thing did not stop, and month after month, all through the autumn and winter of 1864, the tremendous strokes of the Federal battering ram shook the Confederate temple to its foundation. Turret and tower fell in ruins, crushing the gallant defenders, yet the survivors fought on with a desperate valor that won the admiration of fighting men in every country.

Christmas came, but not a glad season; for who can ever forget the dreary desolation that made men sick at heart, and many to wonder if the Prince of Peace had forsaken his people.

"What is that you've brought in that bag, Goodnight, and why are you sticking to it so closely?" asked Joe, on the afternoon before Christmas. He was sitting at the door of his poor apology for a tent thinking of the Christmas time he last spent at Belhaven, when the scout came in from one of his country trips looking in better spirits than usual, and carrying a well-filled sack on his shoulder. Goodnight seated himself on a stump, and, putting the precious parcel under his knees, answered:

"Well, now, Joe, don't you be too perticular. You bet I didn't tote that bag seven miles for nuthin', an' I ain't gwinter turn it loose nuther, with all these rapskalliony fellers a settin' aroun' here with empty stumucks. A empty stumuck, Joe, ain't got enny conshunce, an' I wouldn't trust that bag with the best man on General Lee's staff. There ain't but two men in this army that I would trust it with. General Lee is one, and if I wus to tell you the tother you would feel so proud your close wouldn't hold you."

"Thank you, old fellow; thank you; you make me blush," laughed Joe.

"Yes, I 'lowd as much, but that bag's a prize, I tell you. There's dooins in that bag."

"Dooins?" repeated Joe.

"Dooins, man, dooins! Chrismus dooins, you hear me. Looker here, boy, an' let your mouth water, you hongry young sinner"—and Goodnight drew from the bag the lifeless form of an ancient rooster that had crowed at the birth of the young Confederacy—now to be buried amidst its ruins.

"Now look here agin, will you, an' keep your mouth shet. Ain't them taters about the best truck you've seed since we left Georgy?—but law, they ain't a patchin to what we uster raise in ole North Carliney. I'm that tired of salty bacon and corn bred—if it wernt for the rank pizen of the thing I'd desert an' go over to the Yankees. I lay they'll hev plenty of good things to eat to-morrow; more good truck of one sort an' a nuther, sont from home, than you could shake a stick at. Lawd, Lawd, if we could only git into their camp like we did that Sunday mornin' at Shiloh!—but shucks! I ain't had one dern thing sence I come to ole Virginny but devlish hard knocks, an' plenty of 'em. Now, this old cock here is tuff enuf to hev crowed fer Saint Peter to a wept by, but I'll bile him all nite, an' in the mornin' I'll roas these fellers, an' then—gentulmen, I'm gwinter set down to the best Chrismus dooins in General Lee's army. I'm plum burnt out on bacon an' corn-bred, an' the beef what we gets turns my stumuck. I don't mind the fiten, but this thing of starvin' is agin my principles."

When the scout was in camp Joe got very little chance to talk—once in a while he could get in a question. He now asked:

"But, old fellow, you haven't told us how you came by these dooins; did you buy them?"

"Darnation; no! Buy nothin. They axed me a dollar a pound for some ole flour over there in town this mornin, an' they hed to keep the barrel kivered less'n the weevils would all fly away with it. Buy your granny's milk cow! I conferskated 'em. You know I hes my permit as a scout, but devlish little scoutin I kin do with them Yankee lines only about two hundred yards off from ourn, an' it all open country, too. Then, there's Phil. Sheridan's troopers scourin aroun in every ten-acre lot, ontil a man hes to keep every eye open all the time. One of them blamed fellows got after me one day last week with one of them repetin rifles, an', gentulmen, the way he did shoot wus a caution. I hed to keep dodgin so fast, that I couldn't shoot fer several minits, but bimeby I fetched a crack at him that muster soured on his stumuck. I didn't hev no time to git his weepin; but, here I am, plum off the track. Wus tryin to tell you about the rooster, an' got mixed up with that Yankee. Well, as I wus gwinter tell you, I went back through the town an' over the bridge, an' then I follered a little bline sort of a road

ontil I thought I wus gwine plum to ole North Carliney. I woulder jest nacherly 'er gone on, but, when I
thought about what a hitch you fellers wus all in
here, an' how Gener'l Lee mighter lost heart had I quit
him, I said to myself, says I: Caleb, you've got to dance
to that ole fiddle until the last string pops; an' I'm
gwinter do it, too. Bimeby I come to a little clearin'
on the creek, with a house sot out in the field, an' I
heard this ole rooster crow over in the edge of the
woods. I dunno what he wanted to be crowin fer these
times. I knowd it warn't no use to go up to the house
an' try to make no bargin fer that chicken, so I got me
a good stick an slipt aroun' to whar he wus a
scratchin an' galivantin' about sum hens, an' the
first thing he knowd I wus right on him. He
didn't git out more'n about three kuk-kuk-kuks, an'
made like to run, when I drapt him quicker'n a cat
can wink; I then crawled up to whar they had banked
their winter supply of sweet taters, an' I opened a hole
an' took out as much as I could tote handy, but it did
look so much like stealin that I got out my last five-
dollar bill—new issue—an' fasnin it on a stick, left it
in the hole whar the taters cum from. Ef they don't
spend it purty soon, it's my opinion that they'll hev to
keep it as a war relic."

"Didn't you say you were gwine up to Richmun to-
morrow, Joe?"

"Yes, old fellow; I have an invitation from Colonel
DuPree to eat a Christmas dinner with him to-morrow

evening, and I shall go on the mid-day train, provided our friends in front do not require my attention."

"Well, I never cuss," remarked Goodnight; "but I must say, *dam* a man or a Yankee who won't let a feller live peaceable on a Crismus. Ef they spile your Crismus dinner, Joe, I'll spile some of 'ems supper, or you may call me a Dutchman."

The next morning Joe partook lightly of the "dooins," and, arraying himself in the best of his scanty wardrobe, hied him away to Richmond, and to Jennie As he was about to leave, Goodnight beckoned him aside, and asked: "Is that purty little black-eyed gal of Kernel DuPree's up to Richmond?" And, when answered affirmatively, said: "Tooby shure! I thought so."

When Joe was gone, Goodnight said reflectively: "I knowd it. Nuthin on the top-side of this ole bumshelled earth coulder called that boy away from the front, even for a minit, except that enticin little gal. There never wus but one sech gal made, an' her name wus Susan, and she lived in ole North Carliney."

When Joe reached Richmond, it cost him a ten-dollar bill out of his scanty pay for a carriage to Colonel DuPree's residence. His ring at the door was answered by a smart darkey, who asked, with a streak of impudence, while holding out a silver waiter: "Is you got a kyard, sir?"

"No," replied Joe—picking up a cane that stood at the entrance—"but I have a stick, and I'll break your

head if you don't drop your impudent manner. Go
and tell your master that his friend, Major Mabry, of
the Army of Northern Virginia, is at the door."

The negro jumped as if a ten-pound shell had
exploded near him and rushed to find his master. In
telling his experience that night to his fellows, he
said: "'Fore Gawd! dat young man is a sooner. He
hole he head like he wus a general—rare back like
General Lee heself."

Col. DuPree hastened to the door and welcomed Joe
with the thorough hospitality of an old-time friend.

"Why bless you, my dear boy, I'm truly glad to see
you. Indeed I am; and they tell me you fought your
way up battle by battle until here you are a major at
twenty-one. Well, well, well! I expect to see you in
command of a brigade yet. Ah, Joe! who would have
expected the quiet young farmer boy of dear old Feliciana to become such a superb soldier. Good Southern
blood will tell every time."

Joe modestly disclaimed any merit that deserved a
higher rank, and said that he tried to do his part
wherever duty called.

"By the way, my boy," continued the Colonel, "Jennie is here with me now and as full of life as ever.
These times of trouble don't seem to cloud her spirits
in the least. She went out last night with her cousin,
John Barton, to attend a Christmas festival, and they
did not get home until past midnight, so the lazy little
thing has kept her room the better part of to-day. I
sent her word that you had arrived and she will be

down directly. You and Jennie were great friends in childhood and I know she will be glad to see you. Of course you remember John Barton ; a handsome fellow, so the girls think, though his style of beauty doesn't suit my fancy in a man—a sort of cousin of Jennie's, and very rich."

This last qualification was more powerful with the old gentleman than he would admit to himself.

There was a chill about our young soldier's manly heart at this mention of Jennie and his quondam rival, and, when a moment later the rustle of a woman's garment announced the entrance of that young beauty, there came over him the same feeling that made him tremble when he received his "baptism of fire" that memorable Sunday morning at Shiloh. But only for a moment did he falter—then rising to the full dignity of his young manhood, he listened, while he held her hand, to her stately welcome, so different from that he had dreamed of the night before in the trenches of Petersburg.

"We are all so glad to see you, Major Mabry, and we are proud of your splendid career as a soldier."

Joe murmured his thanks, and replied that the old friends of his boyhood were ever dear to him, nor could he ever forget the fair girl who played and romped with him so long ago.

Other members of the family drifted in, when the conversation became general, and, as usual, the war was the principal topic. It is yet a subject upon which the people of the South love to dwell, for around it

5

cling their saddest and tenderest memories, nor will they ever cease to love and venerate those mighty men of valor who made that immortal struggle the crowning achievement of all the ages.

"Tell us how matters are progressing in front, Major Mabry," said Jennie, "and when will General Lee drive Grant away as he did McClellan and others?"

"Yes, yes, Joe," chimed in the Colonel, "I want to know the honest opinion of a soldier—one who was on the ground and helped to do the fighting. Don't you think the whole business has been miserably botched?"

The young soldier drew himself up proudly, and forgetting that he was in the very presence of "the powers that be"—forgetting that Jennie was listening—told an eloquent story of the wrongs endured by his comrades.

"Colonel DuPree, it will be hard for you to realize that our army is slowly starving and freezing. General Grant need not rush his brave troops against our lines to have them slaughtered, for two months more of such treatment as they have received from the authorities lately will destroy the last hope of the Confederacy. I speak only of material matters now, for there are other things which tend to destroy the *morale* of the army, but this question of supplies and reinforcement is paramount. What is the object of those immense stores in Georgia and Alabama? If they are intended for the army in Virginia they ought to be delivered, or given out to our suffering women and children at home. It looks very much like they were put up as so many baits for raiding parties of the enemy. Do you wonder that our men desert, and that those who once get a chance to go home rarely return? Men may love to fight for their country, and may be drawn by a sense of duty, or a feeling of patriotism, to stick to their post in front, but there are very few who feel called upon to starve in defense of State rights and negro slavery. You may think, sir, that I have picked up some radical notions for a Confederate soldier, but I tell you in all candor that I speak but the sentiments of the men who are presenting their breasts a living barrier to the legions of the North. What is the matter with our people, anyhow? We ought to have a million men under arms, and at least one hundred and fifty thousand of them should be around Richmond, or thundering at the gates of Washington. Now what are the facts in the case? Forty thousand men are all that General Lee can call his own, and they suffering the bitterest pangs of poverty. Think, sir, what they have endured this cold winter, and what they must still suffer on scant rations and not clothing enough to meet the demands of decency; yet they rush to battle and to death with a cheerful alacrity, that proves their earnest patriotism and their glorious courage.

"And our great leader! How shall I speak of him? He stands out the sublimest character in this mighty struggle, and I know his great soul suffers as he sees his men suffer. I tell you, Colonel DuPree, I believe it is the love these soldiers have for that wonderful man that keeps them where they are. They call him 'Uncle Robert,' and no matter how the battle may

seem to go against them, let him but ride along the
lines and it is worth ten thousand fresh troops. They
cannot help from shouting whenever they see that
grand old hero, and the slowest man in the army would
resent an insult to General Lee as he would to his own
father. I love him; yes, you may call it 'hero worship,' if you please; and to win such words of praise
as he gave the young Alabama artillerist I would
cheerfully face the deadliest volley ever poured from
Federal lines. I would even starve for him.

"Now, let me give you, my father's friend and mine,
a word of warning. If you have any preparation to
make for meeting the inevitable collapse, I insist that
you do not delay. The end is rapidly approaching,
and just so soon as the condition of the roads will permit the enemy to move we will be compelled to retreat.
Where will we go? is a question I cannot answer.
The crash will come very soon, but I may not live to
see it. Of one thing I am certain—come fame and
triumph, come starvation and death—I shall follow
'Uncle Robert' to the last ditch!"

The young soldier's eyes were flaming with the
light of battle and his voice was clear as a trumpet.

"Oh, Joe!" cried Jennie, impetuously, "you look
like a hero!" Then, bursting into tears, she fled from
the room.

Joe enjoyed that Christmas dinner, for he brought
with him the appetite of one who had fasted. Jennie
was very quiet, and for many a year she never passed
this anniversary without thinking tenderly of her gal-

lant young lover who came to her from out the din of battle, looked into her eyes for one brief hour, and then rode back into the battle's smoke.

When Joe got back to Petersburg that night he heard the boom of heavy guns and the crash of exploding shells. "Hello, Joe!" cried Goodnight, who was waiting at the depot to welcome his return; "I'm glad to see you back looken so smilin'. Them onmannered Yanks are firin' their Crismus guns, an' being 'feard of wastin' ammynishun they puts in them big shells an' flings 'em over to us with the complyments of the season. Dern 'em! if I don't fling some small-bore complyments back to 'em in the morning, you may call me a son of a Dutchman.

"Lawd! Lawd! I hev spent the miserablest Crismus sence I got through with them dooins this mornin'—sorter sickly about the gills and puny-livered. I reckon 'twus 'cause you went to see that little black-eyed gal o' yourn, an' it put me to studyin' about Susan. I wonder if the good Lord is ever gwinter let me see that gal agin? It'll be jest about my confounded luck to meet her sometime with about six little tow-headed Tar-heels callin' her 'mammy,' an' I can't stand that, nohow. Better be killed by the Yankees. I think, Joe, that I'll get aquainted with some of them North Carliney fellows what's camped next to us, an' maby I'll find some feller what knows the people in my ole diggins; who knows but I might hear somethin' about Susan? Oh, she wus the likliest gal."

CHAPTER XI.

JOHN BARTON AND JENNIE.

ON the afternoon of "New Year's," Richmond was alive with vehicles dashing in every direction. The grandeur, the gaiety, and the wealth of the capital were there, and the poor emaciated private from the hospital was wandering about the streets to gaze upon the festival, and wonder what his wife and babies were doing in the far-away cottage amid the mountains. Who could have imagined that the Goths were already thundering at the gates of Rome, and that the mighty walls were tottering to their final ruin? Yet, with all the signs and portents gleaming ominously along the Southern sky, there was a sound of revelry in many a stately home. Who cared for the distant bellowing of gunboats on the river, and the flaming thunder along the embattled host of foemen? Was not Robert Lee in command? Then all must be safe. Was not the Army of Northern Virginia, glorious as of old, "standing like a stonewall" before the enemy? Alas! the "right arm" of the commander was gone, and his legions had perished by many a rolling river.

A vast cosmopolitan population had assembled in the Confederate capital—thousands of them holding office, and yet other thousands struggling for place.

(102)

On that day dashing young officers and foppish gray-beards—all adorned with gold lace and shiny brass buttons—beat tattoo upon the sidewalks with high-heeled boots, or stormed up the rocky streets in carriages. Were those men rushing to meet the legions of Grant? Ah, no! They were passing from drawing-room to bower, and from bower to salon—with, perhaps, intermediate calls at the saloon. Those men wore military titles suggestive of battle. They are yet "colonels," after a lapse of a quarter of a century, and tell to the present generation many marvelous stories of personal prowess in the old days. They had no hope then of ever winning military fame, unless in the capacity of critics, but the ugliest dandy in the crowd had aspirations to become a drawing-room hero.

Women are the same blessed, mysterious creatures from Boston to Zululand. If they cannot have a man about, they will smile upon a dude. When the man is away off, busy in the battle of life, that nonentity known in all ages as the fop, the dandy, or the dude, attempts the rôle of man, and he sometimes passes current. Is it not possible that the time is coming when the American woman will rather support, protect, and cherish a dude, than be supported, protected, and cherished by a man? The tendency of education is that way.

Late in the afternoon a carriage stopped at Colonel DuPree's gate. A young man alighted with an air of easy assurance, and, dismissing the driver, passed in through the door without the formality of ringing.

He was a handsome young man with shapely hands
and feet, wavy brown hair, and a moustache that the
girls called "just lovely." An elegant Confederate uniform fitted his graceful figure, and there was that in
his movements which suggested "a slight suspicion of
something to drink."

Entering the parlor, self-announced, he found Jennie
comfortably curled up in an immense cushioned rocker.
She hastily folded and hid in her pocket a letter she
had just been reading, and in the depths of her lovely
dark eyes there was a glimmer of tears.

"Ah, my fair tyrant! You needn't hide the letter;
I know it's only a petition from some poor fellow you
have enslaved, and he is praying you to pile on more
fetters. Do I not guess well? Hello! it must be a bad
case, for I see tears in your bright eyes."

"Sit down, Cousin John, and don't be ridiculous.
The letter is from a dear friend, telling me how sadly
our poor boys suffered three days ago during that dreadful snow-storm. The brave fellows were out in the
trenches at Petersburg, and many of them were so terribly frost-bitten that they are being sent up here to
the hospital."

" Yes, yes; that is too bad. We soldiers have a
hard time indeed, and our country ought to be very
grateful. Only the other day, with all that snow on
the ground, I had to go down to Petersburg with a
special letter from the department to General Lee, and
would you believe it, Jennie, I had to ride out three
miles to one of the forts where the General was over-

looking some new works. It was dreadful cold, but the rough fellows were working in the mud and slush, singing and shouting like it was fun. General Lee stood on the ground near them, and they were the happiest men I ever saw. I had to ride out there in an open top-buggy—yes, yes, we soldiers lead an awful hard life."

"Now, Cousin John," replied Jennie, "let me entreat—don't be ridiculous! You talk about a hard life; it amuses me. You spend your time in ease and comfort, and only do a little writing, or riding about. You have the rank and pay of captain, yet you have never been in a battle."

"But you know, Jennie, that I am on General Buffet's staff, and as his business is to plan rather than fight, I am compelled to remain in the city. Somebody has to do the 'head work.' But let me tell you, my bright, guiding star, that I long to rush into the thickest of the fray and pluck bright honors from the cannon's mouth. Oh, if I only knew that you would weep o'er my lowly grave and not forget the young soldier who perished in defense of his country!" Here John grew quite pathetic, and showed symptoms of blubbering over.

"Oh, Cousin John, do stop! I am about to weep now, and I promise you here that when you are killed in battle I'll 'melt mine eyes to tears.'"

John Barton did not know whether to feel tender or savage over this promise, so he returned to the charge:

"By the way, Jennie, who is your tender-hearted friend who writes such a jeremiade about the woes of the soldiers? Strange I never heard of him or met him, since he is such a dear friend of yours."

A flush o'erspread the fair face as she answered:

"Cousin John, you will certainly recollect him—one of your schoolmates in boyhood and now one of the bravest men in the Southern army. My letter is from Major Joseph Mabry."

John Barton was sober in an instant, and an ugly look darkened his face. He tried for a moment to compose himself, but failing to control his passion he turned to the girl and almost hissed:

"Do you mean to tell me that you, Jennie DuPree, are corresponding with that cowardly clod-hopper, Joe Mabry? A fellow whose tastes were so low that he followed the plow and fed the hogs, while I and other young gentlemen rode about the country at our leisure; a fellow who could not dance a set to save his life, and was too cowardly to resent an insult when I threw my glove at his face in your very presence; a clown whose highest ambition was to be called a goody-good boy at school and exhibit prize pumpkins at the county fair. I am astonished at you!"

John Barton evidently did not understand the spirit of his pretty cousin Jennie, else he would have been more diplomatic. The fair girl's face was very pale for a moment, but suddenly the flush of anger mounted to her cheek, and, springing to her feet, the wrathful little beauty astonished him with an answer that he will not forget to his dying day.

"John Barton, stop! You forget that you are in the presence of a lady, and that you are slandering a man whom she is proud to call her friend. A man who is the very embodiment of soldierly valor; whose brave heart has carried him through the dangers and horrors of fifty battles; who has fought his way up from the ranks, and whose lofty soul would spurn the malignant slander of even an absent enemy. O, that my country had a million such sons to serve her in this hour of trial! I would rather be a man and die by Joe Mabry's side in the hour of battle, than be the proudest carpet knight in all this fair city. O, to be a man and a soldier at this hour!"

"John Barton, you did not know Joe Mabry when he was a boy, nor did I. We could not understand how he could work on the farm and yet be a gentleman; could feel an insult, and yet not stoop to the level of a brawler."

John's rare impudence came to his rescue, and ignoring the stinging rebuke of the girl's words, he replied: "Why, Jennie, you are a tragedy queen, and are raising an awful storm on small provocation. This heroic Joe Mabry must have vastly improved in courage since the Valentine party the first year of the war. I couldn't get him to fight then, and you were mighty quick to cut him for a coward. I have always understood that a gentleman would demand satisfaction for an insult."

"Reproach me as you will, Cousin John, for I deserve it all," replied Jennie, sadly. "I have told you that neither of us were able to understand the nobility of soul that characterized Joe Mabry, even in boyhood, and now that he has reached the full stature of a man, physically and mentally, his soul has risen to yet loftier hights. I repeat that I am proud to call him friend, and I warn you now, as you value my respect, to refrain from speaking disparagingly of one whom I regard, and who is worthy of any woman's love. Understand me; I will not listen to one word against my friend. Pardon me, Cousin John, if I have been rude. I had almost forgotten to be a lady."

John Barton did not linger that evening, but prudently took his leave early, and divided his time pretty equally between "hot-scotch" and full-grown profanity.

The winter passed with constant suffering among the troops, relieved only by some terribly sharp passages at arms. Fighting was a relief to those brave men, and they rushed with cheers to meet the attack of the enemy, or sang songs of love and war to while away the hours. The wretched condition of the Virginia roads prevented any very active movements, but the Federal commander was never idle. Vigilant and aggressive, he never lost an opportunity of striking a blow whenever he thought he detected a weak point in the opposing lines. With a powerful army, supplied with everything in the way of equipment; a new man in the place of every one who fell, and a better gun instead of each one lost, there was every encouragement to fight. He did fight with an energy that shook the continent. After tremendous labor, and a display of infinite patience, he succeeded in procuring and mounting a powerful battery of long-range guns on Fort Steadman, and undertook to break the line of communication between Petersburg and Richmond. Shells from those guns did great damage in the city where the marks are yet to be seen, and the effect became a serious problem to the Confederates. General Grant well knew what action his great opponent would take when those guns began to make themselves felt, and like a wise soldier he proceeded to strengthen his works with all the skill known to military science. Not satisfied with the most elaborate preparation in front, he built yet other powerful works within his own lines commanding in both flank and rear his own heavy battery. It was a wise precaution, as the sequel shows, and illustrates the prudence of the man who never failed to accomplish his undertakings. But we will not anticipate, nor will we intrude further into the province of history than is necessary to properly locate our humble characters.

Many of the old soldiers of both sides remember those two rival works on the southeast of the city, grimly named by their defenders, "Fort Hell," and "Fort Damnation." To-day the tourist forces his way through the dense growth of scrub and briars, and walking upon those walls of earth so desperately struggled for, finds in every open space a cankered bullet, or the rusty fragment of a shell—suggestive mementoes of the time

when brother fought with brother, and the saddest
pages of American history were written. So many
weary months of ceaseless watching and fighting; so
much of suffering, of sorrow and of **death**. Alas! for
the brave young men who ended their glorious lives in
this struggle! Perhaps it was best for the permanency
of this great nation that the rich blood should have
been shed. Perhaps to-day when we of the North and
South meet and mingle our tears around the altar of
sacrifice a mutual sorrow brings our hearts nearer to
each other, and may be it was well that the victims
were offered; but ever and ever the suffering soul asks:
"Why was the boy sacrificed? Why was not the old
political ram stretched upon the sacrificial earthwork
instead of freeing his crooked horn from the thicket,
and being allowed to roam the earth at large, vexing
the people with discordant bleating?"

The pines and cherries have grown above the place
of blood, forest trees have sprung from the depths of
the Crater, and the roar of commerce-laden trains sounds
like the far-off muttering of musketry. Lee and Grant
have clasped hands in the spirit world, and a united
band of brothers shout again on the eternal shore.

The gloomy spring of 1865 opened in tears. Kind
nature sorrowed o'er the fate of the heroic little band
in the beleaguered city. The mighty arms of the Federal giant clasped the very pillars of the temple, and
well the defenders knew that when he bowed himself
and put forth his tremendous strength the solid earth
would tremble under the pressure.

Not far to the right of the Crater there is still to be seen the ruins of a covered way which ran out from the main line of defense to the picket line some little distance in front. This ditch passes through one edge of a little country grave-yard, where slept the bodies of a dead and gone generation, and doubtless those poor inanimate pieces of clay kept very still while the tempest of war raged above them.

But what of the immortal spirits? If they come back to earth how anxiously they must have watched the great tragedy develop before their astonished vision! How strange this hurricane of war in a land so peaceful when they left it, and more than strange that its wildest horrors should have centered around that unknown grave-yard. Broken pieces of tombstones lie scattered around, and the stains of leaden missiles still cling to the marble, but the thunder of battle has passed away, leaving no sound save the whistling of the partridge and the cheery song of the plowman.

Here on the afternoon of March 24, 1865, we find Joe in command of the picket post. The pickets of the respective armies did a great deal of fighting in those days, and when properly handled were capable of making a desperate defense of their position. Joe had the remnant of his skeleton regiment, and all the afternoon a spirited interchange of shots had been made with more or less damage. No man could expose his body a moment without drawing a bullet. It was one of those occasions when the shooting appeared spiteful. The riflemen made all sorts of secret apertures in the works where they could fire through without being seen, but not long could one remain in a place. The smoke of his gun would reveal the spot to some **keen** rival eye, and the unceremonious bullet would seek a victim. Joe had brought his boyhood skill into practice, and after detecting several lurking sharpshooters had routed them **out** with a well-aimed ball.

"Boys," said he, addressing those sitting around; "there is a fellow at the end of that log on their line, a little to the left, who shoots with a very close rifle. He put that bullet through Johnnie Stanford's hat an hour ago, and if he isn't scared off he'll hurt somebody this evening. I tried him that last shot and lodged a bullet in the earth just where it joins the log, and I think I scared him, but"——"By George! look at that, will you?"

As he spoke, another bullet came singing past his face and chipped a splinter from the marble that marked the grave of a baby. It was a neat little monument erected by some loving mother years before, when, with tears and heartache, she put her darling away out of her sight. O, little mounds and little marbles! You hide so much that is fair and are so eloquent of love and agony!

"I wish that Goodnight would come; he could stop that fellow's frolic."

Joe had scarcely expressed his wish, when the voice of the giant was heard roaring down the covered way: "Darnation! what do they wanter crowd a man of my size into such a badger hole as this fer? Ef I'd a knowd I hadter git down on my belly an' crawl, I'd a made a run fer it across the open. Confound this hidin an' crawlin, ennyhow—let me stan' up fair an' open an' take a crack at the enemy; then, let him do the same way.

"Hello, Joe! Howeryer, boys? Enny of you dead yet? Ef you ain't, them Yankees hev been wastin a powerful lot of ammynishun, for I've hyeard 'em a poppin away ever since I left the depot."

"We are all right, old fellow," answered Joe, "and are awful glad to see you. We were just speaking of, and wishing for you and your rifle."

"Speak of the devil"—said Lieutenant Featherstone, who lay comfortably behind the little mound, and leisurely puffed the tobacco-smoke above his head— "you know the proverb."

"Speak of your mother-in-law!" growled Goodnight. "You little flap-jack leftenants are too peart, ennyhow. Of all the conseated, imperdent little cusses in the whole world, exceptin, of course, them department clarks up to Richmun—a young leftenant with a little har on his top lip, an' a tin jobstick by his side, is the conseatedest and imperdentest—an' ef you don't like them big words, you kin jest put 'em in your gun an' shoot 'em over to the Yankees."

A general laugh at the expense of the young officer followed this reply; but no one ever got mad at Goodnight.

"Let me give you a morsel of good advice, old coonskin," answered the young man pleasantly. "That earthwork was built to cover men of regulation sizes, and, if you don't squat a little lower, some Yankee bullet will plug that big gourd on your shoulders. We would hate to lose you just now, old scout; besides, it's awful troublesome to bury a big man like you."

Never was advice more timely, and had scarcely been given when Goodnight threw himself down with a growl of rage and clapped his hand to the side of his head. He had just opened his mouth to say: "Confound your advice and you, too"; but he never said it. His tune changed, as he said: "Boys, you're come mighty nigh to a funeral. Ef that feller hader shot one inch to the right, it woulder been good-bye to ole North Carliney. See here where he barked my year."

"By the great hokeys. exclaimed Featherstone; "that Yankee has put you in his mark, my old mountain bull, and he'll claim you on any part of the range. An over-bit in the right ear? If the left has a smooth crop, it's the same mark my father used to use on his calves and pigs down in Georgia."

Goodnight looked at him reproachfully for a second, and then remarked: "Frum the looks of your head, your daddy muster fergot to mark one of his calves— maybe he 'lowd it warn't wuth markin."

"I'll venture that is the same fellow who has been doing such fancy shooting all the afternoon," spoke Joe. "He threw dirt in my face a while ago, put a bullet through Johnnie Stanford's hat, and scared Featherstone out of six month's growth—so I was just wishing for you and your rifle as you came out of that hole."

"Well, gentulmen, ef that Yankee ain't my meat, I'm his'n. I wish you would look at this hearin' organ of mine, Joe, an' tell me if the ole mersheen is damaged much. Now, boys, that is what I claim to be a close call, an' the feller what hes to run sich chances had better keep in a prain' frame of mind. Lawd, Lawd, jest think what a mess I'd be in now ef that feller's aim had been a leetle better. An' I wus feelin' so good, too—hevin' jest heard from old North Carliney. But I'm burnin' daylight, an' now I must 'tend to that feller what put his mark on me. I'll put a brand on him that will erdentify him a hundred yards in anybody's pasture—the sneakin' villun."

The veteran scout examined his rifle, and then working his way on hands and knees about twenty yards further down the little earthwork, he carefully dug a hole through the spongy ridge, making the outer aperture barely larger than the muzzle of his gun. Fixing his huge frame as comfortably as possible in his cramped quarters, he patiently awaited developments; nor had he long to wait, when a puff of white smoke at the end of the log told that another rifle ball had followed its companions on a visit to the party at the little graveyard. In extracting the exploded cartridge the unfortunate sharpshooter extended his elbow for a moment beyond the end of the sheltering log. That one moment was enough. Already the keen eye of Goodnight was sweeping along the deadly barrel, and quick as thought came another puff of white smoke, another sharp report, and there was one more mutilated pensioner upon Federal bounty. A cry of pain broke from the poor fellow as the cruel bullet shattered the bones of his arm, and even as he fainted he heard the tremendous voice of the scout:

"I reckon you'll let us alone for a coon's age! Ef you fellers will quit shootin' for awhile we'll let you take your man back to the hosspital; we've got a little of his smart work to look after over here."

"All right!" came the answer, and between the pickets at this point there was an informal armistice.

CHAPTER XII.

THE armistice agreed upon by the opposing pickets was faithfully kept, and when the stars came quietly out for their nightly vigil the old soldiers, except an occasional sentry, threw themselves down on the earth to rest and to sleep. They lay about in groups, some laughing, some eating their scanty ration, and a few growling over their dismal condition. Soon one by one they went off into happy dreams of home and loved ones. Blessed sleep! where the poor ragged veterans of Lee were fed and clothed abundantly.

Many a brave young fellow dreamed that night of bright eyes that would never more grow brighter at his coming, for 'ere another sun should set his glorious soul would be beyond the stars which then looked down upon him so pityingly Blessed sleep! No thunder of cannon and rushing of squadrons to battle, but beautiful dreams of home and peace.

Our group at the graveyard arranged themselves to get the most comfort, but they were singularly sleepless. Goodnight reclined at the foot of a small cedar that was scarred from top to bottom with bullet marks. Lieutenant Featherstone, the brave young Georgian, lay near the marble pillar that a vandal shell had

broken a few days before, while our Joe spread his
blanket and rested his head tenderly upon the grave
of the baby whose little monument was so cruelly
hacked by the sharpshooter's bullet that afternoon.
No desecration to thee, little babe, for the head resting
on that mound was worthy a laurel crown, and the
heart that beat above thee was faithful to every trust!

As Goodnight settled himself down with a great
grunt of relief he remarked, speaking of the dead:

"These here are mighty peaceable-like nabors we've
got to-night."

"Yes," replied Joe; "the dead never trouble persons whose consciences are easy, and I would that our
friends over the way were as well disposed. I am so
tired of this war—so tired of being cooped up in the
trenches fighting and starving. If we've got to fight,
I want to go out upon the open field and hear the old-
time 'rebel yell,' such as we shouted at Shiloh and
Chickamauga. But let me tell you, boys, that old
shout is but an echo of its former self. The men who
used to follow their bayonets to the music of their own
shouting are dead on a hundred battle-fields, and the
countless thousands who skulk in every swamp from
Virginia to Texas can never be brought to a sense of
their duty. It will soon be all up with us, for at the
rate we are going all will be dead 'ere summer opens.
You know, boys, why we quit calling the roll? It was
so discouraging, and we could count our squads at a
glance. I know that our 'Uncle Robert' will do all
that mortal man can do—more, in fact, than any one

living, but when his soldiers are all gone he cannot keep up the fight."

"I tell you what, Joe," interposed Goodnight, "there are enuf fellers up thar to Richmun', standin' around an' pertendin' to be doin' somethin', to make a peart little army; and I guess it's the same way all over the South. Evry son-uv-a-gun of 'em hes to be fed, too, an' that what makes it so agrivatin'.

"Why, gentulmen, there's enuf of them fellers what rides around all over the country, eatin' up all the vittles they can git, an' plunderin' a little on their own hook, to eat up Grant's whole army. They calls their-selves 'cavelry,' but most fokes calls them 'butter-milk rangers,' an' that name jest about suits 'em, shore 'nuf. Lawd, Lawd, ef ole Forrest could only git holt of 'em he'd make 'em fight, ef there's enny fight in 'em. It's my opinion that lots of 'em are brave men enuf, but they aint soljers.

"What they need is diserplin. No soljer ain't gwinter fight onless you diserplin him, an' the more diserplin you give him the better he's gwinter fight.

"I've been up to Richmun fer two days, an' it fairly riled me to see the 'stonishin ermount of young fellers warin good close—soljer close, too—an 'tendin like they wus doin somethin. Imperdent young devils, too. Why, ser, I wus a walking along the streets a lookin at the sights, (for Richmun is a powerful big town—biggern Wilmington), an' when I got to the Saint Charles hotel-corner, there wus a lot of peart, spry-looking chaps, with good close on, an' their boots jest as shiny as Kernel DuPree's nigger waiter's face—an' what must the pizen young devils do, but grin an' chatter like a passel of young monkeys, an' make remarks about me, sech as: 'Hello, feet! where you gwine with that man?' 'Say, long legs; when'd you come to town?' 'Where'd you git them britches?' An' a whole passel more sayins, sech as no one but a nachell born fool would everer thought of. Well, gentulmen, that riled me, an' I told them they wus a lot of conseated imperdent puppies what hedn't got their eyes open, but, if they'd come out to the front an' fight the Yankees, I'd fergiv 'em. They got hot then, an' wanted to whup me right there, an' one of 'em who had a pore one-legged soljer a blackin his boots, he upt with the little stool his foot wus on an' flung it at me; then, a nuther one pulled out a little pistil about as big as my finger an' pinted it at me. Ef he hader shot me with that thing, an' I'd a ever found it out, I'd a made him think one of them big hammers down at the iron works had hit him, but I jess reached out an' caught the two fightin ones by the collers an' bumped their heads aginst one nuther untel it sounded like two green gourds a poppin together. I then made for a nuther handful of 'em, when, who should cum up but two of them police fellers, with swords, an' tole me I wus their pris'ner. I tole them I reckon not, for the Yankees hed been tryin' that game for four years an' hedn't succeeded yet; but I sed, if I hed done ennything wrong, (which I hedn't) I wus willin to see the generl in charge, but I wern't gwine up before no mayor, nor nuthin of that kind. I tole them I hed a permit from Generl Lee, signed with his own hand—God bless him!—allowin me to scout aroun' when an' where I pleased; that I hed found it convenient to scout about in Richmun, an' there wern't ennybody gwinter stop me nuther, ceppen he wus a better man than I wus, which wern't likely. Well, ser, one of them fellers give the keenest whissel I ever hyeard, an', before you could say 'Jack Roberson,' there wus a half dozen of them policemen all around me. Then I begin to git mad shorenuf. I jess put my rifle down agin the wall, an', squarin myself, I tole them to wade right in; that I wern't gwinter shoot none of 'em, an' I could whup a whole cowpen full of such fellers with my fist.

"Gentulmen, you'd a thought there wus gwinter be the dog-gondest row right there—an' there woulder been, too. I don't know what woulder happened, and how it woulder ended, ef Kernel DuPree hadn't stept up at that minit an' tole them that he knowd me, an' would stan 'sponsible for me; that I wus one of Generl Lee's trusted scouts. There muster been a thousan people around there by that time, an' you oughter hyeard 'em holler when the kernel said what he did— then I felt so good, I hollered too.

"Them police knowd Kernel DuPree, for he wus one of the big guns up in the War Department, an' upon his sayso they let me alone. They'd a better a done it, too; but I wus mighty glad to see the kernel, I tell you, for, if he hedn't a come along, somebody woulder got hurt.

6

"He treated me like the shorenuf white man that
he is, and axed me up to dinner with him.   I despise
a man what will honey about you, an' be so awful
glad to see you, an' yet won't ax you home to dinner.
It makes me think he is a regler ole 'stingy bones', or
else he aint got no good dinner.

"The Kernel wanted to know whar I wus stoppin , an'
he sorter laffed when I told him I wus stoppin' mostly
in the trenches down at Petersburg—that I hed jest
run up to Richmun on a little bizness an' must git
back as soon as possible.   I axed him to show me the
hosspital as I wanted to see a man in there, an' didn't
know where the place wus.   He wus kind, I tell you,
an' showed me 'round to a great big buildin' which he
said wus the hosspital, an' got permission from the man
in charge for me to go through.   After I finished my
bizness there I went 'round to the War Department—
why they calls it that name beats my time.   I didn't
see no cannons, nor no bumshells, nor no nuthin' that
looked like war.   There wus a little army of fellers with
soljer close on, but, Joe, you could take a corporal's
gyard of your regiment an' clean out the hole consarn.
I axed Kernel DuPree what made 'em call it a War
Department, an' he said it wus because they managed
all the affairs of the war.   I then axed him ef the man
at the head of it wus a soljer, an' he said no.   I then
told him that the properest man to run the bizness of
the war wus General Bob Lee, an' ef he hed to run it
accordin' to the ideers of a man who wusn't a soljer
then the whole thing would go a skinnin' up the spout.

He said he wus afraid I wus right, but it wus too late now to change things—although I answered him that it wus never too late to try an' fix things right.

"The Kernel wus so busy that I strolled about the big house lookin' into the differ'nt rooms an' calcerlatin how many stout fellers there wus who ought to be down in the trenches at Petersburg, when I could see the rank young devils a grinnin' an' a makin faces like they thought I wus a whole sirkus. I continued to walk around, payin' no attention to them onery young cusses, for I wus a gittin mighty resless, when who should I run up on but that high-flyin' young feller, John Barton, an' he a lookin' like 'who but him.' He was settin in a nice room with a cyarpet on the floor, an' hed his feet cocked up on a desk smokin' a see-gar"——

"Do I understand you to say that the young man's feet were smoking a cigar, or wus it the desk?" queried Featherstone.

Goodnight rose up to a sitting posture, and trying to smother his indignation, exclaimed—

"Looker here, Leftenant, ef I didn't know you wus a good feller an' didn't mean no harm, I'd fling you over them breastworks. If I didn't I hope I may desert to the Yankees the next minit. Ef you don't keep a gyard on that long tongue o' yourn you'll step on it some day. How's a man's feet gwinter smoke a see-gar? An' a desk? That's one of your fool questions."

Featherstone laughingly apologized, and when peace reigned once more our giant resumed his story.

"Well, as I wus a sayin'—his feet were cocked upon a desk, an' *he* wus smokin' a seegar—dog-gone my skin! who ever hyeard uv sech a fool question? An' to think that a regler fightin' soljer, one of Generl Bob Lee's own men, should a axed it! We'd all better quit an' go home ef soljers are gwinter lose what little senses they ever had. Leftenant, I don't see how you coulder done it. It's amazin'. Now ef it had been one of them clarks up to the War Department it woulder seemed more nacherl like, but fer a regler soljer, who eats gunpowder for breakfast, minny balls for dinner, an' scraps of cold bumshells for supper, it is too redickerlus. I don't see how you coulder done it."

"Hold up, old fellow," interposed Joe, "and don't kick at an innocent little joke. It was all in fun."

"Innercent little joke, is it? and all in fun? All right. As I wus a sayin'——he was cocked up on a desk, an' his feet were smokin—no, the desk wus smokin' a——oh, damn it! you got me so all-fired mixed up, I won't tell the story nohow!"

"Go on, go on!" shouted both the young men, "we are interested and want to hear the whole story." Joe continued: "If Featherstone interrupts you again I'll put him on double duty."

Goodnight's wrath soon cooled down, and he went on with his narrative.

"As I wus sayin, he was—er—well, he looked at me an' called out: 'Hello, Goodnight! come in, old feller, an' tell me all you know in about two minits'—an' if I had, he'd a had to had his head enlarged. He never offered to shake hans, but motioned me to a cheer with a wave as grand as ef he wus the king of Mountezumer.

"'Why, John Barton,'" sez I, "'you appears to be hevin a powerful nice, easy time.'" "'Captain John Barton, at your service,'" sez he.

"'Generl Caleb Knight, at your service, dog-gone you,' sez I, an' with that he laffed an' tole me to set down. I drawed up one of them fancy-lookin' cheers with lion's legs fer feet an' two big long tails stickin' up fer the back, an' seatin' myself close to a desk I cocked up my feet too—but Lawd, you'd a thought there wus a yearthquake! Jest as I throwed myself back to be comfortable an' easy-like the pizen ole cheer give 'way an' down I went on my back—*kerwallux*, shakin' a half bushel of plaster off the ole buildin'. Gentulmen, you oughter heard that feller laff! He like to a busted; but I lipt up quickern you could say '*scat*' and axed him what I owed him fer that cheer. Well, ser, he laffed, an' he laffed, an' he laffed, untel I told him that a feller what could be so jolly these hard times oughter be out in front fightin' Yankees an' livin' on corn bred an' bacon. He sorter winched at that, an' said he wus servin' his country very faithful where he wus, an' onless things wus better managed in front than what they wus he would stay in Richmun. That riled me agin, I tell you, so I up an' told him that all them able-bodied department clarks oughter go out an' fite, an' let wimmen and crippled soljers do

the writin' an' smokin' of seegars; I didn't see no other
kind of work goin' on, nuther.

"Then he axed me how you wus a gittin' along, an'
when I told him you wus gitten so sevigrus that you
wern't happy onless you hed a Yankee every day fer
dinner, he 'lowed you muster improved powerful of
late years. Then, ser, I up an' told him that there
never wus a time, sence you wus knee high to a doodle-
bug, that you wouldn't walk over red-hot grindstones,
barefooted an' blinefold, ef you seed it were in your
line of duty—an' then I hit down on his desk with my
fist, and sez I, ef there's enny man on the top side of
this ole earth that would say that Joe wern't as brave
a man as there wus in this whole Southern Confederacy, with Europe an' other heathen nations throw'd
in fer good count, I would pound him untel he had the
bline staggers. Would you bleeve it, ser, the feller
jess laffed agin an' axed me if I had took a contract to
break up all the furniture in the War Department. He
is that owdashus. I did split the top of his desk, but
they do make some furniture so trifling now-a-days
that it ain't good fer nuthin' but to look at. Gimme
a good hickry chair with a cow-skin bottom, will you,
an' I lay I won't be tumblin' about on the floor like a
great lummux. I didn't stay very long in John Barton's room, for I wus feared I'd break some more furniture, an' I know'd ef he got to givin' me too much
of his slack jaw about the army somebody would hafter
hold me—an' there wern't no six clarks in the War Department what could do it. When I told him good-

bye I 'lowd I reckon he would be down shortly with a musket to run Generl Grant off; but he aint comin'. He told me somethin' about gwine to hell.

"Gentulmen, wouldn't it do me good to see about a dozen of Phil Sheriden's fast-ridin' fellers git after him; but, Lawd! one man would be enuf, an' that with only one leg, too. To hear that feller talk you'd think that Stonewall Jackson an' Bob Lee had both gone to him fer all their war knowledges."

"You don't seem to be very fond of that man, Barton," remarked Featherstone.

"I ain't got nuthin' agin him, but I would like fer him to do some fightin' as well as talkin', an' he'd better tie up his jaw about Joe.

"After all that rukus in John Barton's room, I stood around in the corrydors, first on one foot an' then on tother like an ole gander, an' waited an' waited fer the Kernel's dinner time, 'til the sides of my stumuck wern't mor'n a inch apart. Then, ser, after a spell, when I hed about got over my longin fer dinner an' wus yearnin fer supper, the Kernel come out of his office an tole me it wus time to go up to the house. We got into a fine kerridge an' went a bulgin up the street like we were a goin for the doctor. Bimeby we got to a purty place away up on the hill, with a big house set back in the shrubry, when we got out an' walked right in like it b'longed to us. He showed me into the parlor an' axed me to take a seat; but I looked at the cheers a minit, and then I told him I hed broke all the furniture down in the War Department that a man was

'lowd to break in one day, an ef he had a good strong
stool, or a bench, or a hoss-block, or ennything that
would hold me, I would be thankful to rest awhile.
He laffed fit to kill when I told him what hed happened in John Barton's room, an' goin into one corner
he fetched a little square-looking box of a thing, all
kivered over with flowers an' bumble-bees an' things,
and he 'lowed he reckon that would hold me. He
called it a otterman. I sot down easy-like (of course
you know they warn't real live bumble-bees, or I
wouldn't 'er set on them), and directly that purty little
black-eyed gal come a trottin in an' shook my han',
called me 'Mister Goodnight,' an' 'lowd she wus proud
of me, an' wus awful glad to see me—I know why,
though.

"Ef you beleeve me, gentulmen, I coulder eat that
purty little thing right thar, without salt nur shooger—
I wus so hungry; an' when she said 'Papa, dinner 's
ready,' I jest like to er fainted. Exceptin' of Susan,
there never wus sech a gal.

"May be you think I didn't eat any dinner, calcerlatin' that my mind would er been distracted among
sech grand folks; but you don't know the ermashated
condition of my stumuck. Gentulmen, I fally spread
myself."

"Another triumph of matter over mind," said Featherstone.

"'Tend to your own bizness," growled the giant.
"Who's telling this story, anyhow? Why, Joe, they
did hev the best truck outside of ole North Carliney.

There wus taters—sweet an' Irish; an' they hed ham, man—shorenuf ham. They hed chicken dooins fixed up in dumplins, an' there wus a great hunk of roas' beef that would er fed our mess; turnips an' biled pork, an' hash—Lawd, that wus noble hash! Jest as soft and juicy. Then they hed real flour biskits, of which I et about eleven, an' would er made a dozen, but the apple pie, with happy-day sauce on it, come in jest then, so I wus obleeged to take a fresh holt. Bimeby, when we got through eaten, an' eaten, an' eaten, until you'd a thought we wus fixin' fer a seege, an' I hed to let out two holes in my belt, they brought in some coffee. Gentulmen, it wus coffee, too. No beans, nor goobers, nor parched taters, nor okry, but jest the real stuff that run the blockade from Barzeel, an' cost ten dollars a pound. I do think it was the best stuff—an' then that purty little gal, Miss Ginny, she poured it out—nor she didn't give me one of them little doll cups, nuther; but, Joe, she jest smiled so sweet like an' sed: 'Mr. Goodnight, you soljers are so fond of coffee, I'll give you the big cup.' An' she filled a great big chany thing, all striped and gole, plum to the brim, ser, an' runnin' over. She took up the spoon in the purtiest little white han' I ever saw—not even exceptin' Susan's—an' put in three pilin' spoonfuls of shuger; but, Lawd, man, she needn't er wasted enny shuger at all, fer if she had er jest stirred it with her little finger the whole thing would er turned to 'lasses in a minit. That was a notable dinner, an' when we got through it was plum dark."

Here the giant gave a great sigh of relief, and, happy over the recollection of those good things, turned his face up to the stars and started off into dreams of "real flour biskits" and Susan. But Joe, who could not sleep, inquired:

"Hold on, old fellow—you haven't told us what took you up to Richmond?"

"The kyars, man—the kyars. You don't think I wus gwinter walk all that way through the mud, do you?"

"Nobody but a nachell-born fool would er made sech a answer," drawled Featherstone, imitating the giant's style of speaking.

Joe broke out into a ringing laugh, that echoed across the valley against the enemy's wall and caused one watchful Yank to remark to another:

"Them Rebs would laugh and sing if the last trump were sounding."

"You are even with me now, Leftenant, but I won't hold no malice agin you, for you are a good feller an' a regler soljer. An' Joe, ef you really wants to know what fur I went up to Richmun', I'll tell you now, fer I may never git another chance. You see, it wus day before yistiddy mornin', while I was cleanin' up my rifle and gittin' ready for a scout, a young feller what looked like he wus jest outer the valley of the shadder of death come up an' teched me on the arm, an' sez he: 'Is you Caleb Knight, what used to live in old North Carliney jest before the war?'

"Well, I didn't know what sort of a game they might be tryin' to put up on me, so I answers him sorter cautious like—'Prehaps I mout be an' prehaps I mouten't. What you gwinter do about it?'

"He smiled a sort of a graveyard looking smile an' tole me if I were Caleb Knight, there wus a feller up to Richmun, in the hosspital who wanted to see me, an' ef I didn't come quick it would be too late. When I axed him who the feller was, an' what he wanted, he said he didn't know what the man wanted, but his name wus Pete Brownlow. Gentulmen, you coulder knocked me down with a crowbar, I wus that staggered—but I told the young feller I wus much obleeged to him, that I wus the man he wanted, an' that I would go the fust train. I took the kyars that left a leetle before daylight an' I've told you what took place in Richmun, exceptin' when I wus visitin' the hosspital.

"When I went into the room where the poor feller lay I seed in a minit that the angel of death wus a knockin' at the door. He wus layin' there so still an' pale that it weakened me plum down to look at him, but I walked up to his bed an' he knowed me at once. He helt out a poor tremblin' han', an' to save my life I couldn't help thinkin' of how different it looked from the time he hit me such a dip in the stumuck, but I took holt of it an' told him I wus sorry to find him in such a hitch. He 'lowd he wus glad to see me before he died. I axed him how he knowed where I wus, to send for me, an' he said he had saw me fifty times sence the battle of the Wilderness, but didn't let on that he

knowd me, but now when he wus about to die, he
wanted me to fergive him for the wrong he hed done
me years ago about Susan. I told him I couldn't harbor no resentment agin a man in his fix, an' he seemed
kinder relieved like. Then he told me how he wus led
by his great luv fer Susan to tell her that he knowd I
wer gettin' ready to marry Jane Bridgewater, a long-
legged gal what lived ten miles down the river in Tur-
key Valley, an' wus only fooling with her (as ef ennybody coulder fooled with Susan), but sez he: 'It didn't
do me no good, fer Susan never would listen to me, an'
appeared so mopy an' tired-like as ef she wus waitin'
fer death to come. I kept hangin' about her 'til the
war broke out, an' then bein' desprit, I joined the army
not keerin' how soon I wus killed. I went into battle
after battle, but somehow the bullets didn't tech me
until along about Christmas week, when the snow
storm wus so big I stood on gyard an' didn't have no
overcoat, so I took cold ; and now the fever in my lungs
is a dragin' me off day by day. I hate to die this way,
when it's so easy to die in battle. Don't you remember Caleb, at Cold Harbor, there wus mor'n ten thousand dead Yankees in front of our lines, and maybe I
wus the only man in that battle who wanted to die an'
couldn't, an' agin at the Crater, I wusn't fifty yards off
when men wus tore all to pieces, but the good Lord
knowd best. He hes fergiv me, an' if you and Susan
Warner will fergive me, I'm ready to go.' 'Ain't Susan
married?' sez I. 'No,' sez he, an' ef you ain't a fool
you'll go to her jest as strate as the crow flies.'"

"Gentulmen, I did feel so good jest then that I coulder hollered, but the poor feller watched me so close, an' looked so anxious, that I wouldn'ter give him pain fer a bushel of money. I sot by him after that, but he didn't last long—there come a big spell of coffin, an' then turnin' over on his side I hyeard him give a long sigh an' he appeared to settle down to rest. That sigh muster been his last breath. After a while they put him in a box, an' takin' him in a wagon with four or five other dead men they rolled away to the buryin' ground. After a short time more, when I was a waitin' down at the department, I hyeard a far-away roll of muskets an' I knowd that was the last of Pete Brown-low, until, as the preachers tell us, the great God will come in storms, an' thunder, an' trumpets, an' shoutin' of angels, to call up the dead outer their graves. I tell you, Joe, that ideer of the dead comin' up outer their graves is a strange thing an' makes me tremble. It does seem like some of the poor dead soljers would come up to see how people wus carryin' on in Rich-mun'. They wus a havin' the biggest time the other night at a ball fer the benefit of the hosspital—sech a fiddlin' an' dancin, like it wus in the days of Solermun an' Goliar when the fire and bumshells come down. They'd better be a prayin'."

"Camping here among these graves must have put that thought of the resurrection into your mind, Good-night," said Joe. "That doctrine has disturbed men's minds in all ages, but we need not let it trouble us. The omnipotence of God settles that question in my

mind, and I accept the Bible teaching. It is folly for
me to discard a truth because I cannot fully comprehend it. For instance—we soldiers often see a strong
man fall dead in battle; there is a small bullet-hole
through his body and he lies before us dead. We say
that he is dead. Almost his entire body is as sound
as yours, yet you know he must be buried out of sight
in a little while because of decay. No human intelligence can comprehend the change that has come over
the poor fellow—yet the awful fact remains unchal-
lenged. You say the bullet killed him—but how did
it kill him? A ball has passed through the brain;
yet that perfect foot cannot walk away. He is still
and pulseless. That is what we call death; yet we no
more comprehend it after six thousand years of investigation than did our first parents when looking with
astonishment upon the murdered Abel. Life was there
a moment ago. Three days ago poor Pete Brownlow
was quivering with excitement as he waited for your
word of forgiveness—but now you might shout yourself hoarse, in vain. We cannot understand either life
or death, yet we question neither.

"My faith is very simple. I believe that the all-
powerful God is able to do whatsoever He will with
this poor body of mine. If He has any further use
for it He will take care of it. That is enough for me,
and I feel in my soul that however the end may come,
I will arise perfect in all my parts, ready to answer the
roll-call of eternity, and ready to follow the Great Captain as I have tried to follow our own Uncle Robert."

Joe looked away into the steller depths and wondered if the freed spirit would in its flight beyond those mighty orbits be able to view and comprehend the mysteries of creation; then, rising to his feet, he listened to the boom of heavy guns from the walls of Fort Steadman, and heard the crash of shells falling upon the doomed city. Suddenly he hears the click of a musket and the low challenge of the sentry: "Who comes here?"—and the quick answer—"A friend."

"Advance, friend, and give the countersign."

A young man advanced rapidly, and the words were whispered: "Remember the Crater." Then coming forward to where Joe was standing, he said: "A dispatch for Major Mabry." "I am he," said Joe, and taking the missive he crouched behind the breastwork, where he struck a match and read by its flickering light words that made the blood bound through every vein and thrilled his heart with a soldier's joy.

"CAMP LEE, PETERSBURG,

"March 24th, 1865.

"The Commander-in-Chief has ordered this division to storm Fort Steadman to-morrow morning at 4 o'clock. The Major-General notifies you to bring your regiment to headquarters soon after midnight, ready for action, and relying upon your known devotion to duty he expects you to lead the attacking column.

"JOHN B. GORDON,

"To MAJOR JOSEPH MABRY, "Major-General.

"In front."

Goodnight was sound asleep, lying prone upon the earth at the foot of the battered cedar; but our gallant Major and his brave young Georgia friend were still restless. We cannot tell the burden of their thoughts, but as Joe paced up and down the little path leading to the main line no doubt he thought fondly of loved ones away off in Louisiana, while Featherstone's fancy strayed along the banks of the Chattahoochie.

"You were talking awhile ago about the future of our bodies," said Featherstone, "but what about our spirits? Do you think they linger here on earth amid the scenes of their former joys and sorrows, or have they a 'place of perfect rest—some middle state between earth and heaven? That baby, for instance, whose little grave is at your feet, and the soul of Goodnight's friend, Brownlow, what are they doing? I wish to know, for I am groping and cannot see my way."

"There are many things we would like to know, my dear fellow," answered Joe, "but the knowledge might be hurtful instead of beneficial. The good Book tells us all that we need to know. It is very explicit in regard to the body, also the final destiny of the soul; but we know not whether the latter assumes new and higher duties at once, or enters into a sort of probationary existence until the final judgment. The condition of 'perfect rest' is surely not one of idleness—it probably means entire freedom from all that is hurtful or wicked. A soul with nothing to do would rust out."

"That is all very pretty, my dear Major, but I see you don't positively know much more about it than I do. If the soul has new and higher duties to perform I would like to know where the necessity is for resuming this old body? It seems that some souls have been getting along for several thousand years very comfortably without the incumbrance of the body."

"Why God proposes to resurrect this body I do not know. He made it in his own glorious image and is unwilling that such a work should be annihilated, and when it is raised again, no matter how battered and disfigured here, it will rise 'a 'glorified body,' such as Moses was when he came down from the mount with the radiance of Heaven all about him. But what is the use of speculating about these things? I accept the evidence of my father's and mother's Bible and try to do my duty—may be by to-morrow night, my dear fellow, you and I shall know the truth of many things which are now conjectures. Do you see that flash?— now listen for the roar,"—and it came booming through the night air like deep-toned thunder. "We must silence those guns or evacuate the city. General Lee has ordered our division to storm the fort at day-break to-morrow, and at midnight we are to move into position. Look at these poor fellows now scattered all along the line and sleeping under the stars like they were at home. You disturb them now and in an instant they will spring up, gun in hand, ready for work, but when those stars gleam out once more most of these brave hearts will be forever stilled, and no sound will be able to break their eternal sleep, except the trump that shall awaken us all to a new existence. I examined the defenses at Fort Steadman as carefully as possible three days since, and I tell you, Lieutenant, that the man who marches up to the front of those walls stumbles over his grave at every step. Compose yourself and go to sleep, my boy,—you will need all your strength for to-morrow's battle."

Joe continued his restless walk, until stopping at a little mound where floated a faded banner, he leaned against the staff and looked away to the distant South where the stars were shining so gently down on dear old Belhaven, while Tom was dreaming of battles to be fought and glory to be won.

The great guns had now ceased their thunder and the solemn hush of night had settled over both armies. Only the breeze from the distant Chesapeake moaned through the pine tops or whispered among the sedge, and the hostile warriors were in friendly sleep.

A few minutes later the sentinels of both armies paused on their rounds to listen as a clear voice sang:

"I dream of Jennie and my heart bows low,
Never more to meet her where the wild waters flow."

CHAPTER XIII.

TOM'S BATTERY.

TOM did not go to the wars, but remembering his promise to Joe and heeding the earnest wishes of father and mother, he remained at home and became a very useful boy. Oftentimes as he saw his legs grow long and felt the strength of young manhood expanding his whole frame, the desire to go away and fight his country's battles with Joe became well-nigh overpowering, and in desperation he sought his father one day to beg for that permission, the lack of which only prevented his becoming a soldier.

"Why, father, I can fight and I can shoot as well as Joe ever could, and I know I'm not a coward. See what a famous fellow he has become, and just look how that Richmond paper that Col. DuPree sent you praises his gallantry! He is a perfect hero, and here I am a poor, miserable stay-at-home, with no chance to do anything."

Then the poor fellow burst into tears, and leaning his head over on the table—the same table where the Judge had sorrowed and prayed the night before Joe's departure—he hid his face in his arms. Very tenderly Judge Mabry stroked his boy's hair, and with a father's affection softening his voice responded to this burst of childish grief.

"My son, you are very dear to our hearts, and we would deny you no wish that we think proper should be indulged, but I must continue to be firm with you and control you as I think is for your good. In the first place, you are yet too young, and although as large as many boys of twenty you are hardly sixteen. It is not expected that the children shall fight the battles of this war. In the next place you are doing more good at home raising corn and meat for the army than if you had captured a battery."

At the mention of that heroic performance Tom's tears flowed afresh. "You certainly have not forgotten how General Adams called you 'A gallant young Commissary' when you delivered him one hundred bushels of corn for his troopers last fall?"

"Yes, I haven't forgotten it," replied the boy; "but what sort of cheap praise is that, and who wants it? Might as well have called Uncle Josh, who drove the wagon, 'a noble old bull-whacker.' The war is nearly ended, so you said the other day, and it's all because General Lee needs soldiers and cannot get them. I would rather live one week fighting for my country under him than ten years of peaceful indolence. Why don't men go when he is calling for them so earnestly? Here are these cavalry fellows raring around all over the country and running every time the Yankees come out from the river."

"Hush, my son! You are slandering some of the best and bravest men of the South. All they require is to be taken away from home and given a taste of military discipline. We have found out that men will not fight at home when they can avoid it."

The Judge had stated a truth that military men were slow to learn and did not fully realize until the bulk of the Confederate army was demoralized.

"Let me say further, my son, that if it were necessary for you to go we would not withhold our consent, but you can do no good. If the men are tired of fighting and will not fill up the depleted ranks of the army, certainly the children cannot be expected to do so. Besides, my dear son, I am growing old very fast now and your mother will need your strong young arm to lean upon. You know it will be but a short time when the negroes will be freed, and we will be left with only this worn old plantation, should our conquerors allow us that much; then who will stand between us and starvation should our brave Joe never return? You must recollect, also, that Joe in his last letter urged that you be kept at home."

Tom's vaulting ambition was again brought to earth, but as he left the room he fired this parting shot:

"I was born about five years too late, or I ought to have been a girl "——

Then running out to the stable he saddled young Tudor and rushed like one possessed of a devil away up the road towards the big pasture, and past the tree where he killed his first squirrel. He did not stop this time to admire the famous tree, nor did he stop the fiftieth part of a second as he returned.

If Tom went up the road like one possessed of a devil, he came back in a few minutes like one pursued by a legion of devils, and yelling "Yankees!" "Yankees!" at every jump; nor did he stop at the house, for just as he reached the corner of the yard *pop, pop, pop,* came the sound of a half dozen pistols and a party of Federal cavalry came thundering down the road. Tom's doctrine was not of the "turn the other cheek" order, but "an eye for an eye" pleased him better, and he never received a blow in his life that he did not endeavor to return the favor. He carried in those days one of those marvelous pistols known as the "pepper-box," and it never forsook him in the hour of need. It was the same ridiculous weapon that Mark Twain forever immortalized as "The Allen," and its usual custom was to go off—all five barrels at once. Turning in his saddle Tom pointed the machine up the road towards the enemy and shut his eyes while it scattered five small bullets over the neighborhood. Then he devoted his entire attention to moving on down the road. He never stopped, but clearing a five-barred gate like a fox-hunter, struck out for tall timber with never a thought of glory and no present desire to storm a battery, but full to overflowing with a yearning for the swamp and its peaceful haunts. A few more useless shots at him as he crossed the valley, and the friendly shadow of the forest opened for our young man and took him into its protection, where we will leave him to get over his scare while we return to Belhaven, which for the first time the raiding enemy had reached.

As our Tom's first frantic shout aroused the family, the old cook, Aunt Viney, came rushing in, crying:

"Lawdy, lawdy! Mistis! O, Mistis! Hyonder cums dem Yankees, an' they trineter kill Mos Tom." Then yelling to the passing boy—"Run, Mos Tom, run! dem debbils gwinter ketch you"—she hurried back to the kitchen, determined to hold it to the last extremity. Mrs. Mabry ran screaming to the gate calling on Tom to stop, and crying to the horsemen not to shoot her boy; but Tom never stopped, and the rushing troopers paid no heed to her wild entreaties.

Judge Mabry never lost his presence of mind, but begged his wife to compose herself. "Never mind, my dear,—they cannot catch Tom, and their pistols won't hit him at that distance. Look how he skims across the valley! Ah, he's all right now, and they'll never get him. Did you notice how the young rascal took that gate? If he learns to fight like he rides he will rival his brother."

Returning from their unsuccessful chase after Tom, the party spurred into the front gate, trampling over shrubbery and flower beds with no regret for the wreck they made. We are not inventing a case, but are relating one of the ten thousand mournful incidents of the saddest, wickedest and noblest era of American history. This was only a raiding party bent on plunder, and they put intention into execution at once. Swarming into the house by every door, they were soon working in every room—nor was there a secret place, loft or cuddy, that they did not readily find. It was evident that this force was composed of master builders, or were experienced hands in the business of seeking hidden valuables.

"How are you, old Reb? Ain't you glad to see us?" This was from a burly, red-whiskered ruffian carrying a cavalry saber in his hand, who was the lieutenant in command of the party, and addressed to Judge Mabry, who met them on the piazza.

The Judge replied very politely: "I cannot truthfully say that I am overjoyed at your presence, but I trust that since you are here you will compel your men to behave like soldiers and gentlemen You have the power and I am at your mercy."

"Soldiers and gentlemen, be d——d, old slave-driver! You are a nice looking old cock to be talking about soldiers and gentlemen! We are going to make you help pay the expenses of this war; we cannot afford to tramp around over this country and fight rebels unless we are well paid for it."

"I thought you were fighting from patriotic motives. That is what most of you claim," replied the Judge.

"You thought so, did you? Well, I thought you were old enough to know better. Yes, patriotism is a good thing when it pays. Hand over the keys, old gal"—addressing Mrs. Mabry—"but we really don't need 'em. I can kick a door open quicker than I can unlock it, but it's a pity to spoil the furniture."

"You are very considerate of the furniture," replied the lady, "and I only wish **you** would be equally so in regard to the contents."

"Don't stop to parley, boys; if you listen to an angry woman you will hear something that won't please you. Pitch right in and teach these rebels what it costs to run the country into war." Then followed a scene of indiscriminate plunder and unmitigated deviltry worthy of the middle ages. Trunks, drawers, desks, and every article of furniture were thoroughly ransacked and contents either cast upon the floor to be trampled on, or pocketed for future disposition.

Like most families, the Mabrys had their jewelry, watches and plate safely hidden away, and many a box of silverware in the Southland never saw the light during four years; so, when these ruffians were disappointed in their search they became enraged and vented their wrath upon everything in reach. They mutilated the grandfather's picture by cutting out the nose, and smashed the face of the clock with a tumbler. Some elegantly bound volumes were thrown out of the window to be walked on by the horses, and an antique mirror, set in the wall, was broken beyond remedy. Before long they found a quantity of honest, home-made wine that Mrs. Mabry took great pride in, and then the fun grew fast and furious. One young fellow, who had forgotten his home-training but had not forgotten his music, sat down to the piano and rattled off a lively jig, which started as motley a set of dancers as ever congregated in a Bowery music hall. It was

7

every fellow for himself and old Nick for the slowest. Such a knocking the backsteps and jingling of spurs were never heard in Louisiana before or since. Some of the marks of that day's entertainment may yet be seen upon the floor at Belhaven. Fortunately, they became goodnatured as the wine took effect, and except occasionally kicking an unfortunate chair out the door they broke no more furniture.

Aunt Viney was cooking dinner when they came, and, as we have stated, she entrenched herself in her citadel and prepared to defend it to the last extremity; nor had she long to wait, until a couple of soldiers with the foragers' usual hankering for the cookpot, undertook to capture the fortress. Pounding upon the door for admittance, they heard the old woman's shrill, scolding reply :

" You golong 'way frum here whiteman, an lemme 'lone. I aint gwinter open dis kitchen 'til I gits ready—or ceppen my own whitefokes say so."

"Come, come, don't be so cruel," replied one of the men. " Don't you know that we are your friends and are going to set you free?"

" G'way frum here, I say, an dont you talk to me 'bout no free nigger. Ef you dont go long away frum here I'm gwinter hu't sum o' yer"—came back in warning notes from the kitchen.

"Open the door, you old black fool! If I have to break it down I'll pitch you headforemost out tho window."

"Who you callin black fool, you poor bucra? Cum a hunnyin aroun here an' then like a onmannered critter callin me a fool. My own moster and mistis dont do dat, an' I aint a gwinter 'low no po' white trash to do it, shore! Call me a fool, do you! Call me a fool! You po' ginger-faced yallerhammer!"

A tremendous kick that started every joint in the door followed this outburst, but the blow was not repeated.

"Take dat fer your smartness!" And the irate old woman dipping a quart of boiling water from the pot dashed it against an auger hole in the door, where a great portion of the scalding fluid passed through the opening and fell upon the two hungry men on the steps. The effect was awful. With yells of agony and rage they stumbled over each other getting down the steps, and it was a race to the well, where one plunged into a great tub of wash-water, and the other incontinently rolled into the horse-trough. The victor shouted to them as they ran: "I tole yer you'd better lemme alone, an' you better too! If you cum back here I'm gwinter dubble de dose."

This outcry brought Lieutenant Stubbs and a score of his men rushing from the house, but when they learned the nature of the trouble a wild roar of laughter burst from the whole party, until it seemed more like a drunken Christmas frolic than the uproar of a set of marauders.

Aunt Viney came to the window and holding up to view a smoking kettle said to the laughing men:

"You may laff an' laff til you can't stan up, but you better not cum foolin 'long wid dis chile. I got erbundance of hot water in dis kitchen, an' I'm gwinter make de nabors think we all scallin hogs over here ef enny more of yer try to cum in dat do'—ceppen ole moster or ole mistis say so. You hear my hawn. I'm gwinter do it, sho, an' you better lissen."

"Never mind, Aunty," said the laughing officer. "You shan't be bothered, but you must not scald any more of my men. If you do I'll pitch you into the well."

"Who you talkin 'bout? Me? You gwinter pitch me inter de well? You better try it. You ain't got holter me yit, an' you dasent try it. I dare you like a black dog—I jess dubble-dog dare you! Ef I don't scall the skin offer you thar ain't no snakes. An' don't you cum 'antyin' me aroun here nuther, fer I ain't no kin to you this side o' Adum. I lay ef Marse Joe wus home he'd make you git away from here in a hurry. Well, he would."

"Who is 'Marse Joe,' and what makes him so dangerous?" asked the amused Stubbs.

"Why, ain't you got no sense? Whar you ben livvin all dis time you ain't hyeard o' Marse Joe? He's ole Marster's son—he's oldest son, what's off in de army wid Generl Lee, an' he ain't erfraid o' no Yankee on the topside of this 'uth. Sho-o-o! G'long man. He done kill eleben hundred Yankees wid he own sord, an' ef he cum down here there gwinter be sum more ded Yankees layin aroun waitin fer sumun to bury 'em."

Aunt Viney held the fort until Mrs. Mabry, hearing the controversy and wishing to conciliate the enemy, came out and told her to go to work and prepare some dinner for the troop. The faithful old servant went grumbling to obey this command, for she was still full of fight, and as she busied about her cooking she said to herself repeatedly:

"Well, I ain't gwinter put no salt in their vittles—shore."

While dinner was preparing, the raiders opened the barn and threw out provender for their horses until the whole yard looked like a pen for fattening beeves. Then they prowled about the place or lolled in the house singing and shouting in the very abandon of wantonness.

In the mean time what has become of our young man, whose time to the swamp has never been equalled? When he reached the friendly shelter of that mighty forest he knew that all the Yankees in the State could not catch him, so turning back to the edge of the woods to reconnoiter he saw the enemy riding into the yard and heard their shouts as they trampled into the house. He had in a measure gotten over his scare, which was mostly the result of surprise, and now hot, indignant wrath took possession of his soul. Shaking his fist towards them, he exclaimed:

"Oh, you thieving devils! To think that I had to run like a coward the first time I ever met the enemy.

But I'll get even with you before the day is gone if I have to follow you clear to Port Hudson. My promise is no longer binding. The war has come to me, and now I propose to strike one good blow for my country if I never get another chance. If I can only find Captain Ransome in time we will make you shout another tune—you plundering rascals!"

Then turning his good pony, Tom cantered away through the woods to a cow-ford across the creek, when he plunged through and hurried on to the hills, where he hoped to find his friends in camp. He was not long in reaching the spot where the gallant captain, with his scout of twenty men, was resting after an all-night tramp into the low country. Tom galloped right into the arms of a vigilant sentry, who pulled him up in short order, with the remark:

"You seem pushed, young man. Where are you going in such a hurry?"

"I am looking for Captain Ransome. The Yankees are just back here at Judge Mabry's, not more than three miles, and you may have heard their shots. They fired nearly a hundred times at me as I ran, but it takes a fast bullet to catch this pony."

"Hadn't you better come down a bullet or two, my lad? A hundred shots ought to have aroused us even at this distance."

"Well, I'm certain they shot at me," replied the boy, "and if they had fired a thousand times I couldn't have run faster. I did my very best and have hardly stopped running yet."

"Ride right in, my son, and you will find the command just over the next hill by that little spring branch. Don't rush into them too fast."

Tom hurried on and was soon in the presence of a splendid loking young officer, who listened to his story with great interest, nor did he delay action, for a minute later the stirring notes of the bugle called to arms.

"What is the number of the party?" inquired the Captain, but Tom could only guess.

"I cannot say, Captain, for certain, but from the looks of the party as they swarmed into father's front gate, I should judge them to be twice as strong as your troop—may be fifty men—but, pshaw! Captain, your squad ought to be able to whip three times their number of Yankees any day."

"My dear boy, your war experience is very limited. I shall not shrink from a conflict with double our number of the enemy if I can get any advantage, but man for man the Federal troops will give us all we can attend to. We will have to be cautious in this case, but no matter how strong they are we must give them a brush. You can pilot us the nearest way I suppose?"

"Yes, sir. I know every acre of these woods. Many an old gobbler I've 'yelped' around here in the spring time, and I know I've killed a thousand squirrels among these hills. I'll show you the way, that is what I came for, and if you'll let me I'll take a hand in the fight, too. They shot at me first awhile ago, confound them! and I want one good fair lick at them."

"All right, my boy. We have a spare pistol, taken from the body of a negro trooper—a black Yankee—killed in a little affair down on the Port Hudson road, yesterday morning. We struck a party of about thirty of the black rascals gathering in the stock at the Barziza place, and were right on to them before they knew it. We had the most delicious bit of fun I've experienced since the war began."

"I reckon you hurt some of them, Captain"—suggested Tom.

"Well, yes. Some of them likely never knew what hurt them, for my men carry sharp sabers, and I doubt if more than half of them got back to the fort. We certainly gave twelve of them their freedom—you probably know that we never take negro prisoners. By the way, are you not the son of Judge Mabry, where we took supper last night? We are under obligations to you for the way you poured out the corn to our horses; the poor beasts were sadly in need of supper."

"Yes, sir, I am Tom Mabry, and while I've had no chance to fight Yankees, I've fed many a good Confederate's horse when mother was feeding the rider."

"The good lady and your excellent father treated us so kindly last night that it will be a great pleasure for us to help them to-day, when they have fallen into trouble. Come, I see the command is ready, and we must be riding.

Away they went trampling through the forest until the sound of hoofs died away in the distance, then the wild hogs came stealthily out from a neighboring thicket and took possession of the abandoned camp, while the squirrels and jays chattered and scolded from the overhanging boughs.

Tom, as guide, rode beside the leader, who listened with kindly interest to the hopes and dreams of the impulsive boy, and smiled at his extravagant ideas of life on the tented field. When they reached the brow of the last hill ere they should plunge into the deeper shades of the valley there came a mighty roar, like the explosion of mortars at the great bombardment. Involuntarily the entire troop halted.

"Is that a cannon?" asked Sergeant Graham.

"Yes," replied the Captain, "but it is heaven's artillery, and we have no call to attempt its capture. We have been counting it on our side all this time, although I have good reason to think that we may have been mistaken."

In the dense shadow of the forest, where the foliage almost shut out the light of day, they had not observed the sudden advance of one of those summer tempests so common to our southern latitude until they were alarmed by its opening gun.

"We must hurry," said the Captain, "and get into the low grounds, where there is less danger from the lightning. These lofty trees upon the hill-top will bring down the bolts upon us"—even as he spoke a mighty chain of fire rushed down to the earth, and in its progress shivered a giant poplar to the roots, hurling fragments of many hundred weight in every direction; then, while their eyes were blinded by the flash, there came upon them an awful roar of thunder, so appalling that men involuntarily shrank from a power they could not combat, and the frightened horses dashed madly forward in vain effort to escape the tempest.

"Forward, men!" shouted the Captain. "To the shelter of the valley!"

The command hurried on rapidly, but ere they passed the slope the great fountain of the skies burst forth and the water came down with the rush of a cataract. The howling of the wind and the swish of escaping waters were enough to confuse the strongest men. Again and again the clouds parted, riven asunder by the fiery stream that poured upon the trembling earth with a roar like the trumpet of judgment, while the wind bore upon its wings all the screeching demons of the air. Great sheets of water, like sea-waves picked up bodily and broken into fragments, came breaking and crashing through the groaning tree-tops, and as our party scrambled into the valley they found a flood gathering to stay their progress.

"Make haste!" cried Tom, "or the creek will be past fording ere we can reach it."

Being measurably protected from the wind, they spurred forward and plunged into the rapidly rising stream—the last horse swimming as they reached the further shore. Almost as suddenly as it came, the tempest passed on bellowing into the low country, and as the rain ceased the whole party drew up upon a little knoll to rest a few minutes and arrange their further progress.

"It is only a mile to the house, Captain," said Tom, "and if you will follow this path it will bring you into the road about half way. That is the same road you travelled yesterday evening when you visited there, so you will know the way."

"What is the matter with our young guide?" asked Captain Ransome. "You surely don't mean to desert us just as we are about to strike the enemy?"

Tom's face flushed at the suggestion, but he replied steadily:

"You mistake me, Captain. I am ready and anxious to fight those fellows with you, but I want a gun that will do some damage. This pistol is probably all right, but you never know who you are going to hit with it, and it's an accident if you don't bring down your next-door neighbor. The trifling rascals fired at me to-day several shots at less than one hundred yards, and did nothing but scare me half to death. About a half-mile below here on the bank of the creek, in a big hollow beech tree, I have a shot-gun hidden away. I keep it wrapped in oil-cloth to protect it from damp, and it is one of the best weapons of any make for close range. I hid it and other valuables, away out of reach of both Yankee and jayhawker, so if they catch me they won't get my gun. The boys all call my gun 'Old Eternity,' and whenever she calls something has to answer. I have her loaded with a double charge of powder and twenty-seven blue whistlers in each barrel, so I think I'll feel better with my old friend than depending upon this popgun. You go ahead, Captain,

and I'll catch up with you before you get to the house.
If I don't my father will disown me."

So saying, Tom put spurs to Tudor and was soon lost
to sight in the dense forest.

Speed, Tom, speed! The hour has arrived of which
you have been dreaming since you first begged to be
allowed to go to the war with Joe! Urge the good
pony to his best, Tom, and be careful how you ride!
Boy, do your best, for upon your puny arm depends
the issues of life and death, and the minute has nearly
come when your glad young voice will thrill the souls
of despairing men like the note of a trumpet! Be
true, old gun, for never did your deadly barrels look
to fiercer game than awaits you this afternoon!

"Look to your arms, my men!" came the quick
command 'See that they are dry and everything in
order. If those raiders are not careful we will surprise them in the midst of their deviltry. I expect
you to follow me, boys, and we will strike one good
blow for our country, even should it be the last."

Away then, as fast as the nature of the ground would
permit, they sped in search of the enemy. The clouds
were passing off and the glorious sunshine came drifting down through the treetops forming transient jewels
of the million rain-drops hanging to the leaves. Bird
after bird fluttered the moisture from its wings and
joined the forest chorus, while the glorious afternoon
was filled with melody. Since the storm had swept by
the day seemed too calm and peaceful for battle, and
riot, and sudden death; but the savage that is in man

breaks out as fiercely on a May morning as in a December night.

Our scouts hurried on to battle, and as they marched Sergeant Graham asked: "Do you think we shall see that young man again?"

"I am certain of it," replied the Captain. "I don't think I can be mistaken in his determined look and manner; yet, if we are to have hard fighting I would rather know that he was out of it. A little touch of a skirmish, and let him get a couple of shots with that remarkable rabbit gun of his would please him and square his account with the enemy. I shall expect him."

If our Captain calculated to surprise the enemy he was mistaken, for Stubbs was an old stager who had seen much hard service in Kentucky and Missouri, and he had long ago learned, by sad experience from the hands of a party of Forrest's men, that the soldier who relaxes vigilance in an enemy's country is a candidate for misfortune. The raiders were already in motion, coming leisurely down the road in front of Belhaven, both horses and men being full of good cheer and plunder. Stubbs, feeling superlatively jolly, had broken out into a song, and with a tremendous bass voice was making the woods echo with the doubtful melody of—

"Katrina and the big bologna sausage,"

but just as he approached the end of the avenue and the poor lovesick Fraulien—"Avay to der kitchen she ran"—there came the sharp crack of a dozen carbines, emptying several saddles, and throwing the entire party into the utmost confusion. Back rushed the front of the column, and after them, with wild hurrahs, came the little band of scouts, under the lead of the gallant Ransome, firing their pistols as they came. Several more saddles were emptied, and it looked like sudden destruction had come upon the hilarious crowd; but Stubbs was no coward, and the most of his men had tried their courage on many a well-fought field.

"Halt, my men, halt!" he shouted. "Are you going to run from a scouting party of a half-dozen rebels like a pack of cowards? Turn about and show them that soldiers will fight! Follow me! Down with the rebels and rally round the flag!" Then, throwing himself at the head of a dozen of his men who had recovered from their surprise, and shouting to his sergeant to rally the remainder, he formed across the avenue and met the charge of the scouts with a rattling pistol fusilade that did some damage, but could not stop their headlong career.

"Give them the saber, boys, and crowd them before they can rally!"—shouted Ransome, and bursting upon them like a tempest, horses and riders rolled in the mud. One brave fellow fired point blank at our Captain's face, the bullet fanning his cheek as it passed, but ere he could amend his shot a keen saber went crashing through his skull, and he sank utterly dead into the ditch that bordered the avenue. Stubbs fought with the strength and courage of a desperate man and more than one scout gave back before the terrible blows of his vengeful sword. He had beaten down the guard of Sergeant Graham, breaking the saber of the latter smooth off at the handle; the flashing steel was about to claim its victim, but even as in fierce joy it descended, it glanced in a shower of sparks from the blade of a master, and he met the eyes of Ransome, aflame with the light of battle.

"Dog of a robber!" shouted Ransome.

"Death to the rebel!" answered the undaunted Stubbs, as he whirled his saber with tremendous fury. But he had met a saber that never yet acknowledged a superior, and it required all his skill and immense strength to parry the blows that rained upon him. The fighting became desperate and brutal at this point, but now the rallied troopers of Stubbs's came thundering up from the rear and by weight of numbers pressed the scouts back, still fighting furiously. The two leaders were separated in the mêlée and each shouted encouraging words to his followers, while their sabers found abundant work in the general engagement.

Ransome soon found that he was being overpowered by the great number of the enemy, and as several of his force were already down, he saw with troubled heart that he must retreat to the shelter of the woods or be destroyed. Slowly and sullenly he drew back, followed by the shouting enemy, until he reached the end of the avenue, where he determined to make one more desperate stand.

Even as he turned to meet the exulting foe in one last despairing struggle he heard a boyish voice call to him:

"Be ready, Captain.   'Old Eternity' is going to hurt somebody."

Then from the end of the avenue hedge came a roar like the report of a mountain howitzer, and a perfect tempest of buckshot swept the road for two hundred yards.   A wild yell from the scouts hailed this new ally.

"Give it to them again, Tom!" shouted Ransome.

When again with tremendous boom the old gun hurled its contents, and before it both horse and rider went down—while behind it, from the force of recoil, our Tom measured his length in the mud.

The blood-thirsty Stubbs fell at the first fire, and but few escaped a wound amid that rain of bullets.

"Look out, boys!   An ambush!" cried one of the raiders.

"They've got a cannon!" shouted another.

And dismayed at the unexpected enemy and the fall of their leader, the panic soon turned into a rout.

"Give them the saber, boys, but spare those who surrender," was the command, and away they went up the hill past the house they had so lately plundered. Throwing away their burdens as they ran, and trusting to the fleetness of their steeds, the routed raiders fled before the sword, while fast upon their heels came the vengeful scouts.

And who should be in the lead, upon a swift pony, but our Tom?   Back over the same road the pursued of a few hours before was now the pursuer, and his being the only loaded pistol he was popping away at the fugitives every jump.

Up at the house the family were intensely excited when they heard the conflict in the avenue, but when the fleeing enemy came hurrying by in wild confusion their joy knew no bounds. Aunt Viney was still mad, and when the fight commenced she seized her kettle of hot water and made for the front gate, where she took her stand, determined to make it hot for any one who tried to enter. When the rout commenced she couldn't stand still.

"Hoo-e! Jes-s-s look at dem Yankees! Fo de Lawd, Mos Joe muster struck 'em! Look at 'em, Mistis, how da're gitten over dubble trubble! 'Pears like da muster struck a whole biler fuller hot water down dare an' da's huntin' a mill pond. Da cum a gallupin' up here fo' dinner *terplockety, plockety, plockty*, an' now da gwine back *kerbookety, bookety, bookety*, da lebble tipt end best.

"Lawd! Lawd! If yonder aint sum of weall's fokes a cummin' after um like a black runner after a lizzard! Look at dem swodes, will yer? In de name of de chillun of Iserl, who dat shootin' so big? Jess lissen at him, peepul! *Kerbow! Kerbow!* law, law! Cum here an' hole me, peepul! Ef dat aint Mos Tom on young Tudor! Look at dat chile, willyer? *Kerbow! Kerbow!* Um-m-m-m. Peepul, lissen at him shoot!"

Then the faithful and excited old creature began to sing:

"Run nigger, run, patterroller ketch you!
Run nigger, run, it's almost day;"

and actually danced about the yard until she brought on a case of what Tom called "colored hysterics."

The horses of Ransome's party were too tired from the fatigues of the day, and the long scout from which they had just returned, to allow them to follow up their victory. Besides most of the men had received cuts, bruises, or pistol shots in the encounter, and all were worn out with riding or fighting; so after pressing the flying foe well on to the river road, they returned to Judge Mabry's to look after the wounded and bury the dead.

Stubbs and one of his followers were found lying within twenty steps of the place where Tom opened on the party with his artillery, and the unfortunate musician was stretched out at the foot of a water-oak with a bullet through his brain. Five dead horses and eleven men were lost to the enemy in this desperate little battle; also seven troopers badly wounded. There is no telling how many suffered, as Tom's showers of buckshot swept the avenue in succession. It was like shooting into a flock of blackbirds. Captain Ransome lost three killed and several more were suffering from severe wounds. Five prisoners were captured and quite a lot of plunder recovered, including three of Judge Mabry's mules, and his stove-pipe hat, which one laughing young devil had worn off cocked rakishly on the side of his head, but which he was glad to abandon in his flight. The victors went into camp under the great beeches in front of the yard, and Aunt Viney was again called on to cook for soldiers. In her enthusiasm she salted the supper twice and forgot to replenish her warlike kettle. Every few minutes during the operation of cooking, the old woman would have to stop and call some one to hold her while she gave vent to her joy and astonishment at Tom's remarkable performance.

"Who would ebber 'spected dat chile do so big, an' he aint hardly done waring long shuts, nuther. Law, law, peepul! Dat chile muster loaded his gun wid bilin' water—an' den see how he cum tarin' up de road like de dogs was after him, a hollerin' an' a shootin' at dem Yankees like who but him!

"Man, ser, ef dat boy hader had a swode dare would-enter been not one o' dem Yankees left. He'd a fally skarified 'em, he would. Shoo—g'way from here all you niggers, fer I'm gwinter make dat chile de bigges taterpone ever was made on dis plantation, an' I aint gwinter stint the sweetnin' nuther. You hear my hawn!

"Lawd a mussy! Lawd a mussy, on dem poor ded white mens down in the abenue. Dare po' mammys at home gwinter weep an' moan an' 'fuse to be cumferted. Lawd a mussy! Lawd a mussy!"

That night after supper Judge Mabry and Captain Ransome had a long conversation regarding the war and the enlistment of Tom. The Captain begged that he might have the stout boy in his command, and promised that he would look to his welfare as he would for a younger brother. "Besides, my dear Judge, after the affair to-day your boy will not be safe at home. If those men should get hold of him they will shoot him without mercy, for he has no protection under the rules of war—not being an enlisted soldier."

"I must consult his mother," replied the Judge—"although I know you are correct, and I will give you an answer in the morning."

Tom heard this conversation and his heart leaped within him at the prospect of satisfying the taste he had that afternoon acquired for war—yet how often are we doomed to disappointment. The cup comes close to our parching lips sometimes, but is dashed to earth ere we can satisfy our longings.

When the next morning's sun arose in splendor upon the Southland, the smoke had cleared away from its battlefields, and the long agony was over. Who is it that rides past the dead men in the avenue, and hurries with jaded steed up to the gate at Belhaven? You may weep tears of vexation and sorrow, Tom, for the courier who comes announces the surrender of Lee's exhausted army, and a cessation of hostilities. You may weep, Tom, for tender women and strong men are weeping all over the land.

Yours is a sad case, Tom, for with your record of romantic daring and unselfish devotion to the South, you will never be enrolled

A CONFEDERATE SOLDIER.

CHAPTER XIV.

" FERGIVE ME, JEDGE—I' VE COME BACK ALONE!"

THERE are days in our lives that we look back to with a strange fascination although the memory of them comes up to us through a mist of tears, and the burden of an old time sorrow grows heavy again.

We often forget our joys, and the recollection of many of our happiest hours grows dim as a dream of the night, but never can we put away from us the dead body of some old day which shall haunt us until the grave hides us and our griefs.

Such a day was the 25th of March, 1865, and although the passing years have brought to our Tom sorrow after sorrow, mingled with joys innumerable, again and again comes up the memory of that fateful day. So with Jennie, when in the stillness of some summer night she sees the flash and hears the far-off roar of the tempest, there comes to her the shadow of a grim fortress with deep-voiced cannon, where in the early morn was heard the last triumphant shout of a vanished nation. For one heroic hour the brother and lover was seen breasting the storm of battle, then the pall of smoke came down and loving eyes could see no more.

Promptly at midnight the remnant of a famous regiment marched quietly back from its post on the picket line and directed it's course to division headquarters. Here it paused while arrangements were being made for the final movement and Joe hastened into the presence of his commander.

That officer was seated in his tent examining some drawings when Joe entered. He looked up quickly, and exclaimed: "Come right in, Major Mabry! You are always on time when there is work to do. I am pleased to find you so prompt."

"Thank you, General," replied Joe, saluting. "When we know our duty it behooves us to be in line promptly. General, please allow me to express to you my gratitude for this latest display of your kind confidence. Such an honor rarely falls to the lot of a young man, and I shall endeavor to deserve it. I am twenty-one to-day, General, and I could not celebrate my majority better than by doing some good deed for my country."

" Noble words, young man, and may God keep you for your country's sake! I know that I can depend upon you and your men to stand firm under the critical pressure of the first fire. So many troops who are brave enough after the battle is once well joined, shrink with a panicky feeling from the expectancy of waiting, and it often ends disastrously, when it should be otherwise. I will not conceal from you that you go into the very face of death, for the fort is very strong and will be bravely defended."

"I know that, General, for I have examined the works and can observe no weak point, but the danger cannot be greater than the honor. I am ready."

"You but increase our estimation of you," said the General. "Colonel Grace, your late commander, who has been absent on sick leave, has not recovered. His old wound received at the Wilderness is troubling him again, and his furlough has been extended indefinitely. To-morrow, you, my brave boy, shall wear the star of a Colonel, and I wish it were possible to fill your depleted ranks."

"General," exclaimed the blushing young soldier, "you are too kind, and the authorities are giving me more than I deserve. I fear I shall not be able to meet your expectations, but I will try. Let me go now, if you please, and talk a little while with the brave, patient fellows who are to go with me—you know they must help me win my star."

"Go, with your General's best wishes. You have your instructions. I will see you again at sunrise in Fort Steadman."

Out into the darkness of the night, and into the heavy mists that were sweeping up from the ocean, our Joe took his way to where his little band of heroes were resting and waiting for the hour of conflict. Calling them about him he told them of the danger into which he should lead them, and what their country required at their hands.

"It is unnecessary for me to tell you, my brave men, that I know you are ready to go with me, for you are always ready when your country demands a sacrifice at your hands. I have seen this heroic old regiment gradually melt away under the fierce heat of battle

until now you are but a remnant—yet such a remnant
as the soul of a warrior burns to lead. I came to you
when torn and bleeding you stood like a rock in the
Wilderness. I was with you on that dreadful day at
Spotsylvania, when a continent reeled under the shock
of battle. At Cold Harbor I saw your front a blaze of
awful carnage as the enemy went down before your
guns. I saw you spring to your feet undismayed on
that July morning when a volcano burst under our
lines, and I heard your fierce shouts as you swept the
foe into the Crater with your bayonets. I have seen
your brave comrades perish in a hundred struggles,
and together we have suffered the pangs of cold or
hunger all through the fearful winter. We are now
about to make one last supreme effort. Death is in front
of us, but we have gotten used to him. His terrors are
only for the coward or the guilty. Brave men know
how to die, and where to die. I will not ask if you are
ready to go where I shall lead. I know you are ready."

A low murmur of voices, whispered almost, yet
heard beyond the stars, answered:

"We are ready!"

"Very well," resumed Joe. "At 4 o'clock we will
pass beyond our lines and rush upon the enemy's
works. Until that hour make yourselves as comfortable as possible, and be strong for the battle."

Joe then called Goodnight aside, and together they
talked long and earnestly.

"My faithful old friend," said Joe, "before we go
into this fight I want to ask you to take upon yourself

the burden of certain commissions. You know we are going into a place of great danger, and death will find many of us. We may neither of us return, but should you escape and I not come back, I want you to take my sword home to Tom and tell him to keep it as stainless as when he receives it. Tell him that Joe never forgot his cheerful little brother, and that he has ever loved him with a brother's love. See my folks in dear old Belhaven, and tell them that although I may have passed out of their lives I would have them ever cherish the memory of their soldier boy. And dear old father! I wish I could hear him read from the Gospels once more, and then listen for the rustle of angels' wings as he prayed. Let mother know that the little Testament she gave me always goes with me to battle, as a messenger of peace amid a world of storms, and tell my sweet sister that her lover is safe to her now, but in her joy she must not forget the dead brother.

"And now, Goodnight, one more commission and I am done. You know there is one whose love I have sought since I was a boy in the dear old home. She has always been very shy with me, and sometimes she has wounded my heart; but that was before she knew me. If I should die to-day I think she would sorrow for me. Ah, if I but knew that. I have no word for her, but you may tell her to accept my last exploit as a message. She will understand it."

"Looker here, Joe," interrupted his faithful friend. "I don't like to hear you a talkin' about dyin'. Why, boy, ain't you been in a hundred battles, an' ain't you

8

walked where bullets were fallin like rain, jest like you wus kivered all over in steel an' didn't keer what it rained? Don't talk to me 'bout bein' killed—you rile me. I'll bet you six months' pay agin a ginger-cake that you'll come through all right an' that you'll marry that purty little black-eyed gal in less'n a year. It makes me weak about the gills to hev you a talkin' thet way, an' I don't like it. How am I gwinter fight less'n I keep up a good heart? Of course, Joe, I'll tell your folks all about you in case there's any necessity for me to do it, but whose gwinter tell Susan that I died fer my country when I'd a much ruther went back to her? S'pose some fool Yankee weighs my shugar fer me."

"My dear old fellow," replied Joe, "it is not in your line of duty to go on this expedition, and I do not intend to allow you to be present during the attack."

Goodnight sprang up from where he had been sitting and exclaimed:

"Oh! you don't, don't you! Well, beggin' your pardon, fer I'm talkin' to Joe now—not to Major Mabry—how you gwinter keep me from goin'? Jess so shore as you lead this ole piece of a regiment against that fort at 4 o'clock, or any other hour, jess so shore is Goodnight gwinter take a hand in the rumpus! I think it dangnation mean of you, Joe, to wanter leave me behind, an' ef any man on this green earth had o' tole me you would treat me so, I'd a upt sir an' called him a liar—I don't keer if he wus as big as the sons of Enock. Joe, you don't mean it, an' it aint pos-

sible nohow.   I've been with you in a hundred scrapes
an' waded through some of the biggest battles in Tennessee or Virginy right along by your side, yet now
when it comes to runnin' over a little bobtail fort what
I could take a good runnin' start an' jump plum across,
you want me to stay back, because you're 'fraid I'll
git popt over with a bullet—I jest aint gwinter do it.
You know very well that I promised the Jedge, an'
your good mammy, to take keer of you, an' I mean to
do it to the best of my sarcumstances.   I reckon I'm
your Gyardeen, appinted by your daddy an' mammy,
an' ef a Gyardeen don't outrank a Major, then I'd like
to know what a Gyardeen do outrank."

"My old friend," said Joe.   "You know that I have
loved you since I was a boy, when we used to hunt
wild ducks together in the Comite swamp, and I tell
you now that my manhood strength has not outgrown
that love.   Didn't you carry my heavy knapsack for
me on that awful march from Shiloh back to Corinth ?
Haven't you stood guard in my stead time and again
when I was so sleepy that exhausted nature could not
be aroused ? Whose bullet was it that stopped an enemy
trying to shoot me at Murfreesboro' but yours, and
whose strong arm was it that rescued me and carried
me off from the fatal Mission Ridge ?   Ah, Goodnight!
you have proven youself my friend a hundred times,
and now I want to show my friendship for you by de-
tailing you for other service this morning."

"It aint no use, Joe; I'll jest disobey orders and risk
the consequences.   These here are dreadful times, Joe,

with nothin' to eat an' old Death so busy that he is a pintin' every one of his fingers at somebody; so I'm bound, accordin' to promise, to stick to you. I do hope, my boy, ef there's a bullet moulded for you the good Lord will turn it to'ards me, fer I aint got nobody to be sorry when I'm gone, an' I aint useful like you. But man, man, we're gwinter hunt the game agin in that old swamp when them blamed Yankees quit huntin' us. We'll have sech a huntin' frolic when we git back, that your grandchildren will hear 'bout it."

Suddenly the order came to advance, and silently those brave men passed outside the fortifications, leading the way—into the jaws of death. The attempt to surprise the Federals was only partially successful, for ere they had traversed two-thirds of the distance there came the sharp report of a rifle, followed in an instant by a tremendous boom of cannon, and a storm of grape-shot swept over the head of the advancing column.

"Forward!" cried Joe; and with a shout that drowned the rattle of musketry four thousand Confederates swept up to the fort and over its walls like a great inundation. It was in vain that the suddenly awakened Federals endeavored with the utmost gallantry to defend the works. Officers threw themselves sword in hand upon the line of bayonets and perished in the struggle. Artillerymen died at their posts while loading their guns, and many a brave fellow from beyond the Potomac rose up in the early light to sink back into a darkness upon which no sun would ever rise.

Side by side Joe and Lieutenant Featherstone mounted the parapet, and there with the shout of battle upon his lips the heroic young Georgian fell with a bullet through his noble heart. Joe saw his comrade fall, and at the same moment he observed an artilleryman endeavoring to fire upon the crowded assailants one of those big guns which had brought on this attack. Quick as thought he sprang to prevent the shot; there was a flash of bright steel in the morning air, and the unfortunate gunner went down beneath the stroke. Wild with triumph, Joe placed his left hand upon the coveted gun, and waving his sword shouted:

"Forward, my brave boys! The fort is ours." Then suddenly staggering back he leaned upon the gun and would have fallen, but a strong arm caught him, and a kind voice murmured: "Oh, Joe! I do hope you aint hurt!"

This was just at daylight, and the tide of battle swept on heedless of the wrecks in its path.

An hour later the gallant Gordon led back the remnant of his column, torn and bleeding, and as he passed the now silent gun he saw sitting beneath it a desolate man holding in his arms the dead body of a young officer.

"Alas! It is my brave young major." And tears came into the eyes of the great soldier as he stooped above the heroic boy. Then he thought of his midnight promise, and tearing from his own collar a glittering star pinned it upon the young soldier's breast, and the ragged old veterans saluted the dead colonel as they passed.

There amid the very wreck of battle Joe won his last title.

"Oh, Joe! Joe! They can come now with their stars an' proud words, but you don't know it, an' you won't answer your ole friend enny more. Why don't you open your eyes an' speak to me, Joe? You don't hear me, Joe? It's your own ole Goodnight what's talking to you. Oh! Lord God Almighty! I can't think about Joe bein' dead. Why didn't you take me an' leave this blessed boy?" Thus wailed the tender-hearted scout, and as the Federal troops resumed their place about the recovered guns their leader saluted the heroic dead and spoke kindly to the grief-burdened prisoner.

"Let me bury my dead," said the poor fellow, "an then you may do with me what you please."

After a promise to make no effort to escape, the good soul secured some rough boards from an abandoned barn, and with the aid of such tools as he could borrow in the fort he soon constructed two boxes, and then with patient labor dug two graves at the foot of an ancient pine, which then stood a little distance in the rear of the fortifications. When the great sun was sinking to rest beyond the distant Appomattox he laid the brave young Colonel and his no less gallant friend down to that sleep that shall know no waking until thunders mightier than those then shaking the walls of Fort Steadman shall bid the dead hosts arise to meet the Prince of Peace.

Alas! that our Joe should have given his young life in vain. For when his patient old friend smoothed the lonely mound above his head those great guns were tolling the brave boy's requiem, and his matchless leader was preparing to leave the fated city.

*   *   *   *   *   *   *

The bravest note in our song of war is lost, and henceforward there will be something missing from its music which no tale of love, or joy, or sorrow can replace; for Joe, the matchless young patriot, is dead and the faithful Goodnight is fretting like a caged eagle behind the bars of a distant prison.

Who can tell the sad longing and tearful waiting in the far-off home when one by one the stragglers returned, yet never came the form of the boy so loved? Many were the fruitless inquiries made by Judge Mabry and Tom for news of the missing one, and the gray hairs of the old father grew whiter under the torture of suspense.

Week sped after week, and the war was ended. Then the prisoners from the forts and islands of the distant North began to return, but still no word of Joe, until one day towards the end of June, when at its close the family of Belhaven were assembled at the evening meal, there crept in at the front gate a weary, ragged, and wretched man, who staggered to the door, and as he fainted away through hunger and exhaustion, cried:

"Fergiv me, Jedge. I've come back alone!"

CHAPTER XV.

MADGE.

THE old church where the committee that wrestled with Goodnight had been so informally appointed was a notable landmark in the hill country. Here, on two Sabbath mornings of each month, winter and summer, from generation to generation, the good people for many miles around used to assemble, and if that old house was not one of the gates of heaven, it was at least a resting place just outside the gates. Some of the good old men and women were seen there for the last time, and afterwards when inquiry was made for them, answer was: "They have passed into heaven." That good place must have been very near.

Of course some persons went without any very definite idea of worship, and with others the intention to worship was perhaps secondary, but one thing we are sure of—there never was a more orderly congregation, nor more profoundly attentive, since the mailed hand of Miles Standish enforced Sunday discipline around Plymouth Rock. No whispering, nor the smallest ghost of a laugh, and if our Tom used to peep over his hymn-book in the direction of Major Carter's pew, he was like the ancient Joey B., "devlish sly."

Those Sunday mornings were "seasons of refreshing" to the entire community. All the boys and the young men, also most of the dignified gentlemen of middleage, road horseback, and came upon the ground early. The gentlemen of the South rode fine horses in those days, and they rode with skill and grace. When the men and boys were assembled—generally an hour before preaching—they collected in groups upon rustic seats beneath those noble old beech trees and discussed the events of the week. From time to time as the later arrivals came up there were the cheeriest and friendliest greetings that ever fell from kindly lips upon grateful ears, and if there were any heartburnings, bickerings, or jealousies, our Tom cannot now call them to mind. He was rather young and inexperienced then to observe such things. He was a greathearted fellow who loved the whole world, especially one little blue-eyed maiden, and never dreamed that the world could be in any other condition of mind or heart.

There were no politicians in this Arcadian community, but the people were all intelligent, well read, and thoroughly alive to the rush of events. Of course, those ante-service meetings under the greet trees were not entirely free from political discussion, but the venom was all left out. Judge Mabry was an old-school Whig, while Colonel DuPree was a loud-talking Democrat; yet they were able to parry and thrust without even a bruise. If the discussion became too warm for the day and the place Uncle Billy Farmer would hurry into the church, and as he seated himself in the amen corner his trembling voice would sound

the opening notes of that grand old country church
song:

    " How tedious and tasteless the hours."

Dear old Uncle Billy! Your kindly voice is hushed
to mortal ears, but we will all hear it again where
"Ten thousand times ten thousand, and thousands of
thousands" fill eternity with music.

No subject was ever so earnestly and exhaustively
discussed under those noble old beeches as the crops,
and especially was cotton a never-ending theme.
During "thirteen months of the year" it required
work, and needed to be talked about. It was fresh
when remarks about the weather became stale. "Are
you done planting? Did you get a good stand?
When will you finish scraping? Have you run round
your cotton yet? What about the boll worm? What
make of cultivator do you use? Will you use a sweep
or a twister in that sedge cut? Is your cotton shed-
ding much? What about caterpillars? You will
begin to pick next week, won't you? Will you commence ginning before November? How many bales
have you sold, and what did you get?" On and on,
never tiring, rolled the volume of questions to the
exclusion of many a subject of nearly equal import-
ance. Some men could think of nothing else. The
boys used to tell as a joke on old man Pennyworth, a
rich old five-hundred bale nabob, that his regular
Sunday morning greeting to Colonel DuPree was:
"Good morning, Colonel! How is your cotton?"

It would be amusing reading to tell the hopes and fears of boys about the age of our Tom when waiting under the trees they would catch the distant roll of a carriage. How their young hearts fluttered with eager excitement as carriage after carriage turned the bend of the road and thundered up to the front of the church. How grandly that pair of grays tossed their heads and lifted their feet as if disdaining the earth they walked upon, and conscious of the precious burden they drew.

With what a lordly air old Cato used to leap down from his lofty perch in front, and with an old-time bow open the carriage door for the ladies to descend ; then with what an easy, jaunty air one of the boys would step out from the crowd to assist the ladies, and how, despite his enforced *sang froid*, his heart was all in a flutter and his walk decidedly uncertain. It is astonishing what a small root, pebble, or unevenness of surface is sufficient to trip a healthy sixteen-year-old boy under such circumstances, and then what an amount of blood rushes to his face, while his ears burn and his tongue trips in sympathy with his feet. Don't laugh at him, please, but consider how honestly he is trying to be polite.

But here comes a noble pair of bays, with harness always black and shiny, with carriage ever seeming fresh from the shop, and driven by an ancient darkey whose good-natured face betokened the kindly soul within. Ah, yes! The shiny old carriage and sleek bay horses, with the antique driver, still linger in Tom's memory, and he would recklessly exchange four hundred years of the future if he could go back over twenty-five of the past; if he could see again—the old darkey with his carriage and bay horses? No, no. These were but followers in the train of the princess whose blue eyes and sunny hair are ever present amid a thousand bright and tender memories.

Tom fell in love early, and we might add—often. Somehow or other, nor can we explain the philosophy of it, boys who are fond of fishing are equally fond of the girls. Probably they are fond of most good things. Perhaps the fact of lingering along the banks of a creek in the pleasant spring-time, and having to be quiet a few consecutive hours, have a tendency to develop the love-germ that lies hidden in every heart. You get a good, healthy boy quieted down for a few days, and the little god will mark him for his own. Our Tom was a tender-hearted fellow, and no pretty girl could escape being loved by him. We have known him to love several girls at once, and this we ascribe to his abundant heartfulness rather than to mere wantonness—an effort to dispose of his vast wealth of affection. But the day came when he was about the age of sixteen that brought with it a little princess who was easily able to monopolize Tom's entire capital, both principal and interest, together with all that he could borrow from a score of passionate poets. She came to school one bright winter morning, and bankrupted him in five minutes.

Tom had known her from infancy, but had not been thrown much with her for some years, so now he was all unprepared for the vision of loveliness that made the winter day seem a morsel of spring-time. Life suddenly passed above and beyond the dull reality of "intransitive verbs" and "promiscuous examples," quickly becoming a thing of dreams and beautiful longings. If the boy's lessons were learned that day it was because he was ashamed to miss them in the hearing of Madge, and when at recess he renewed acquaintance by presenting her a mammoth russet, which he had kept hidden away since the October harvest, his tongue faltered and his ears burned as they had not since the last application of the maternal hand. His strength utterly collapsed when his sister Janet cried:

"Just look at Tom! Oh, fie! See him blush because he gave Madge an apple."

Tom suddenly thought he heard a call from one of his chums out on the ball ground, and answering: "Yes, I'm coming," hastened away, while Madge and Janet made merry over the apple. Never was there a happier boy than Tom during that session of school. It was generally understood among the boys and girls that Tom and Madge were sweethearts. She loved to play with the big boy who was so tender with her, and so mindful all the while of her pleasure; while he—well, Tom was foolishly in love with the pretty little maiden, and woe to the unlucky schoolfellow who made faces at her or flipped paper balls at her across the school-room when the teacher's back was turned. He was just as certain to feel the weight of somebody's hand as Madge was to scold Tom for fighting.

The springtime of 1865 will ever linger in our memory, and in every history the reader will find a leaf turned down to mark the culmination of tragedy. Tom was happy in the ever-smiling presence of his little Princess, and grew anxious waiting for tidings of Joe, who had disappeared in the wreck about Petersburg. He was but a boy, and had a boy's light heart, although the entire land was groaning under the accumulation of woes. His lessons were so much pastime, and his hours of freedom were a murmuring brook of pleasure. He would gather the prettiest flowers for Madge, and for her the beech-limb swing was entwined in the shadiest nook. To him she was the fairest, daintiest creature that ever bloomed with the flowers, and we shall ever think that a girl should be counted fortunate who possesses the first worshipful love of an honest boy heart.

A boy loves spontaneously and unselfishly. There are no considerations of fitness or advantage, but the love just wells up in his heart, regardless of surrounding, as the pure waters of a spring gush from the earth—sometimes to catch the sunlight in marble basins, or maybe to trickle away and be lost amid ooze and brambles. It is a fair pearl that is often neglected amid the sparkle of diamonds, and is cast out to be trodden under foot, but the boy love remains to make the man purer and better through all the coming years.

People often laugh at the boy, and call his pretty attachment "puppy love," when, in fact, he is absorbed in the master passion of his life, and will never again thrill with that divine essence which makes the world an eden.

When the weather grew warm the school children discarded the more active games, such as "cat," "town-ball," and "bullpen," for the boys, "kingbase," and hopscotch," for the girls, contenting themselves with those old time amusements called "marbles," and "mumble-the-peg"—the children said "mumbly-peg."

Boys did not go around with pockets full of little black allies making life a burden with their eternal rattling, but with round honest taws played square honest games, with no suspicion of "keeps" or any other specimen of juvenile gambling. The nearest approach to gambling that we have any recollection of in those days was a game called "hull-gull," or "jack in the bush," which was usually played with chinquapins, and was not really bad, for both of our boys used to play it. In the game of marbles a big fat fellow graced the position of middle man—a much more innocent creature than the middleman of whom our farmers complain to-day— and to plump him from taw, a line about twenty feet away, was worthy to be called a game. Perhaps no game in all the list of boyhood amusements appeals so to our hearts as we advance in years. Doubtless many a digni-fied Senator or Governor of to-day would swap all of his honors to feel once more the long ago thrill of a school-boy game of marbles. Above and beyond the tenderest

love passages, or the consummation of political hopes,
rises the memory of that old game, and no man is ever
so dead to his boyhood that his heart fails to quiver
when he hears the well remembered "ventyer roun-
dance!"

If our Tom dearly loved to fish, and if he fairly
adored Madge, he thoroughly revelled in a game of
marbles. To him it was the acme of human amusement, and if he had no white companion to play with,
Black Dave or Bowlegged Bob were just as skillful as
their white playmates and even more anxious to play;
so he rarely suffered for a game. The girls used to
take part in those games, and they were adepts—some
of them. Tom was a champion in the marble ring
and wore his honors proudly, but in manipulating the
knife through all the twists and turns of mumble-the-
peg Madge knew no superior. The boy who played
with her had, in schoolboy vernacular, to "eat dirt."
A peg driven into the ground by three well-directed
blows from a knife-handle in the hands of a vigorous
girl is not readily drawn with the teeth, and Madge
could drive the peg about as well as she could manage
the game.

One delightful day at dinner recess—and no other
day was ever half so fair—she challenged Tom to a
game, which he without a moment's hesitation ac-
cepted and rushed heedlessly on to his fate. Any other
boy on the face of the green earth would have done
likewise. At her bidding he would have attempted
things more impossible than winning from her a game

of mumble-the-peg. Can Tom ever forget the wide-spreading beech through whose dense screen no sun-ray ever pierced, and the little mossy knoll where that fateful game was played? Not if he should live a thousand years. He played that game faithfully and honestly, but he was beaten. He never can forget how with his own pocket-knife the fair little hands shaped the peg, how the blue eyes fairly sparkled with fun, how she rested her tuneful little tongue in one corner of the rosebud mouth, and how with mischievous energy she drove the peg home at two blows. He begged and was granted the unusual privilege of cutting a hole beside the peg for his nose—for Tom's nose was not the least interesting feature of his face. Then stooping to pay the forfeit he found—not the peg, but two girlish hands hiding it from his reach.

"Indeed, Madge, I shall!" exclaimed Tom, trying gently to push away the hands.

"Indeed, Tom, you shall not!" was the laughing reply. "I just wanted to punish you for being so proud of your marble games."

Tom seized the hands, and in the struggle the pretty face was close to his. The laughing eyes looked exultingly into his soul and thrilled him beyond resistance. What would you have done, kind male reader, had you been in our hero's place? A thousand to one that you would have acted just as Tom did if you have a heart in you as large as a marble. You couldn't have helped it.

With all his boyish love lighting up his face he kissed the sweet, laughing mouth, and then blushed, boy like, at his own presumption. Madge had been kissed a thousand times before, for she was a most winsome little creature, but not that style of kiss. It was the kiss that is never repeated—the first love-kiss. It was love's first and sweetest expression. It was heaven.

Madge flushed like the sunrise as she drew away her hands, and exclaimed:

"Oh, Tom! how could you?"

"Madge, darling, how could I help it?" answered Tom.

And then she ran away to the school-room, leaving him with a buzzing sound in his ears and the notes of singing-birds in his heart, while he looked too foolish and happy for expression.

CHAPTER XVI.

"THERE NEVER WUS SECH A GAL AS SUSAN."

AFTER the burial of the two young soldiers the poor heart-broken scout was sent away to Fortress Monroe, where he remained until the final liberation of prisoners early in June, when he was turned loose at the gate of the fort without a cent in his pocket and but a few days' rations to support life upon the long journey he at once began. Wearily he toiled along the road from day to day during the sultry summer time until he reached the pleasant mountain regions of his own dear old "North Caliney." Here he looked upon the mighty hills and clear rushing streams until his soul was filled with a great joy that for a time almost obliterated the sorrow of the past few months. Like a dreadful and beautiful dream seemed the years when the continent rocked under the trampling hosts, and often at night by some lonely camp fire the old warrior would start up suddenly to answer the call for battle, then he would look around for Joe. Poor fellow! It looked like the Lord God of Hosts had forgotten you, old scout, but you were not alone in your desolation. The agony of that time is yet painful, and many a gallant heart will yet go sore to its grave.

But our giant was getting home again. Was going back to the graves of father and mother; back to the pleasant scenes of his boyhood—and to Susan.

There was no poorer and more utterly disconsolate creature on earth than the paroled Confederate soldier who trudged the long journey afoot from Virginia to a desolate home in the farther South; yet, like Goodnight, he took heart as he neared the old familiar haunts, and the world has never seen a more glorious super-structure than sprang from the bitter ashes of 1865. The indomitable courage of a hundred battle-fields blazed afresh upon ten thousand cotton-fields, and the skill that reared those immortal lines of defence has plucked from the deeper earth its mineral treasures, or set in motion countless scores of spindles. Victory has grown up out of defeat, and to-day that poor half-starved "rebel" of twenty years ago stands in the halls of Congress a leader among leaders. So much for heroic endurance South—so much for manly forbear-ance North.

Our friend Goodnight felt his heart grow light within him and his step more elastic as he approached the old neighborhood, and so kindly did he feel towards all the world that when he met "poor little fool Si Owens" in the road he could have hugged him then and there. Not being recognized by that old-time mouse, who had "laffed and laffed" when he gnawed the lion's meshes, he did not make himself known, but passed on up the familiar way until he came to the Warner place, and with trembling heart walked into the house—right into the presence of Susan.

"Oh, Caleb!" exclaimed that impulsive young lady —"you have come back to me after so many years!"

"Yes, Susan, I've come back, an' God help me, we won't misonderstand each other no more."

Into those strong arms all covered as they were with rags, went Susan, and never woman rested her head upon manlier bosom or heard the responsive breathing of a more faithful heart. A few short hours of love and rest, then our scout rose up renewed in strength and made ready to resume his journey.

"Oh, Caleb! Must you leave me and so soon?" wailed Susan, now loath to loose her new-found lover.

"Yes, dear. There are them what's waitin' to hear from that brave boy who died in these arms, an' I must keep my promise to him. Unly a few weeks, dear, an' I'll come back as quick as the kyars can bring me. I have no money an' I must walk like I did when I went to Luzyanner first, but I know they'll help me to git back. The good Lord never made better people than them what I lived amongst."

He then told her of his good friends away off in the South, and of his noble young fellow soldier whose dying words he was to carry to waiting hearts.

The girl listened with tearful attention while Goodnight told her of those who had befriended him, and of his love for the heroic boy. Then drying her tears she said:

"Caleb, of course you must go without delay, but you must not go unprovided. You must have some money to help you on the road, and here is what I have. It is all that is left of the small sum given us by father when he died two years ago," and the loving girl handed him a little netted purse in which jingled a few of the old-time dollars of ante bellum days.

"I can't take it, Susan, for you will need every dollar of it, an' I can work my way. No man ever yet starved in this country, an' I can walk my thirty miles a day. Maybe once in a while some of the railroads will give a old soljer a ride."

But Susan, not to be outdone, insisted that he must take a few dollars to use in case of extremity, and yielding, as the lover always does, he put into his pocket six half-dollars, and vowed he never was so rich in all his life.

Away then upon his long journey sped the faithful fellow, and be it said to the eternal honor of an impoverished people, that he never asked in vain for assistance. Many a friendly "lift" in carriage, wagon, or cart did he get for maybe ten or twenty miles, and once in a while some kind railway official "passed" him a portion of his journey. His poor, tattered attempt at a gray uniform, and his honest face, won his way where even money could not carry him, and more than one aristocratic mansion opened wide its doors to shelter the weary soldier. Often at night, when sitting upon some country piazza surrounded by kindly hearts, he told the story of his mission and the tragic fate of our young hero, tears of sympathy flowed, while many a sorrowing mother thought of her own lost boy. Thus on for three weeks, until near his journey's end, he put forth all of his enormous strength, and after clearing forty miles fainted upon the threshold of Judge Mabry's residence.

No need to tell of the kindly hands, both white and black, that bore him away to bed, nor of the tender hearts that yearned in sympathy over the poor broken-down soldier. Enough that he wore the color so dear to every heart, and ten thousand times enough that he was Joe's comrade in time of battle and had held the dying boy in his arms. It required no words to convince the family that Joe was no more, for well they knew that only death could part the noble scout from the boy he loved so well. The great dread that for three long months had hung like a cloud over fair Belhaven was now the sad reality of woe, and words are idle to attempt the story of that time of sorrow. The patient old Judge would sit for hours by his favorite post on the front gallery, looking away down the avenue where his son had ridden out of sight just four years before, and as the blessed tears came to soothe his suffering heart he felt in his soul the peace that is beyond our human comprehension. Tom wandered about over the plantation seeking for something that was lost, and ever as he wandered there would come up to him a refrain from that sad little song:

"Oh, call my brother back to me!"

Then there came over him an uncontrollable desire to go again to the well-remembered haunts where he and Joe spent that last memorable day. He strolled away to the creek where they fished so happily on the day that heard the first gun at Sumter, and he

listened while the musical waters still rippled over the
log where Joe caught the famous trout, but in vain he
waited

"——— for the touch of a vanished hand,
    And the sound of a voice that is still."

There upon the smooth bark of a great holly that
stands upon the bank of the creek were the carved ini-
tials "J. M." and "J. D." The letters were dim to the
boy's vision that day—dimmer than now when the
mosses of twenty years are clinging to the bark. Wherever he went there were things to remind him of Joe.
Upon that mighty oak Joe had killed six squirrels one
autumn morning, and the great magnolia spreading
above the spring branch had sheltered a gobbler that
fell before the boy's unerring rifle. What boy besides
Joe had the nerve to climb the old tupelo in the
slashes for the vagrant coon? Upon the base of a
lightning-blasted oak that stood just beyond the sedge-
field were traces of a fire the boys had kindled one
winter night when hunting with Uncle Zeb, and upon
that log they were seated while the old man told them
a marvelous story of a catamount he had conquered in
the long ago. Tom seated himself where Joe had
rested, and scratching down to the root of the tree found
ashes—but not fresh ashes like those then gathering
about his heart. At every step something sprang up
to claim a sigh until he hurried home for sympathy.

Since that sad day the resistless years have thundered by building up and pulling down mighty
empires; the waters have worn away the log where

Joe caught the famous fish, and the attrition of many a winter's rain has brought the hillside sands to fill the lurking place of the trout. Tom's raven locks show the pale touches of sorrow, the memory of Joe is still fresh under the burden of more than twenty years, and the boy love for his big brother has never grown old.

When Goodnight had sufficiently recovered his strength and was able to come down to the sitting-room the family were all assembled to hear him tell his story.

'You know, my friend," said the Judge very solemnly, "what we are waiting to hear." There was a painful pause of a few moments while the scout tried to press down a lump that would rise in his throat, then he began:

" Oh, Jedge! It breaks my heart agin to be here in his old home an' know that his bright face is gone from us forever. I thought durin' the time I wus in prison, an' durin' my long journey here, that I hed sorter got over it; but Lawd! Lawd! it all comes back to me so strong that I aint a man enny more."

Here the brave fellow burst into tears, and for a few minutes there was no sound save the sighs and sobs of mourners—then bowing upon his knees the aged father lifted his trembling voice to Him who wipes away all tears, and once more in that blessed old room there was the rustle of angel wings while the comfort of the Holy One came down into every heart.

9

"I wish I could tell you all about him," resumed Goodnight, "but I aint got enny fine words so as to give you
enny ideer what a noble fellow Joe was. He was always ready to do his duty an' no man ever had a kinder
heart in his buzom. When it come to a fight he wus
one of the certenest men you ever seed. He would jest
clinch his teeth an' wade right in no matter if it wer
rainin' bullets, an' when he come across a wounded
inemy he wus jest as kind as if it was his own brother.
He never did luv the war, but he was into it for all it
wus wuth, an' if General Lee had o' told him to take
his regiment an' go up to Richmun an' clear that War
Department plum out, gentulmen, he wouldn't a left
hair nor hide of it—woulder jest nachully a tumbled
every one of 'em into the Jeems river. Oh, he'd a done
it! When he wus in camp he never would fergit me
an' if he didn't hev but t · taters for a day's ration he
would save one of 'em for me, thinkin' maby I'd come
in offen a scout hongry—but Lawd! I warn't gwinter
go without feed if there wus ennything to be had. I
ingenerally picked up lots of truck o' one sort an' a
nuther out in the country an' was more likely to have
sumethin' for him."

Goodnight never tired of telling about Joe's battles,
or of his days and nights in the trenches. He would
dwell with animated face and voice upon the story of
Shiloh, Murfreesboro', Jackson, Chickamauga, Mission
Ridge, Cold Harbor, Spotsylvania, and all those fierce
fights about Petersburg, but ever as he came to that

last sad morning he would think of some other detail of camp life or some other story of battle.

"But I must come to the last an' tell you how me an' Joe parted company."

Then he detailed all the incidents of that talk under the stars, and of the last wild struggle. How they rushed over the walls and bayoneted the defenders at their post; how as the bright sword flashed in the early light the cruel bullet did its work, and how with the name of father and Jennie upon his lips the young soldier turned his brave face up to the brightening east and died with a smile.

"God forgiv me, but I did rebel agin his decrees right there, an' I did think it wus cruel to let that boy be killed, with me left livin right along side of him. Oh, Jedge! You orter seen him when he put one hand on that big cannon, an' wavin his sword—his face lighted up jest like the flash that was comin all over the east, an' he shouted as clare as the sound of a rifle on a frosty mornin. Then when I caught him in my arms he jest smiled as peaceable like as a child, an' he said:

" Goodnight, the war is over an' I'm goin home.'

"Then he shet his eyes like he wus gwine to sleep. Torectly I put my hand on his side an' felt fer his heart, but it wus still.

"Them Yankees wus jest as kind to me as if I'd been one of their own men, an' when they got back to the big gun whar me an' Joe wus and seed their men layin dead as thick as leaves, they wus sollum, I tell you. The officer in charge of the gun wus jest as tender as a 'oman, an' helped me lay Joe out in a blanket; then he showed me whar to git some tools fer makin a coffin and diggin the grave. He come back to that big pine tree whar I wus diggin, an' when I wus plum tired out he took holt with his own hands an' dug like it wus his own friend he wus workin fer. He b'longed to a New York regiment, an' when I went off to prizon he took charge of Joe's sword an' said I could git it when I wus exchanged. I told him your name an' whar you lived, so he could put it down in a little book, an' if he lives you'll hear from him some day."

Thus ended his sad story which he had traveled nearly a thousand miles to tell; then the old scout lingered for a week or more with his good friends. Before he left he went over one day to pay his respects to Col. DuPree, and tell Jennie of her lover's last hours.

The news had already spread, and of the fate of the young soldier Jennie had heard. This was but confirmation of the dread in her heart that had lain there since during those awful last days in Richmond she had heard that Joe was missing. Our tender-hearted scout was melted again when the proud little lady came into his presence. Poor Jennie! Her false pride had vanished in the presence of her love. When Goodnight had told her all and come away she knew what the dead boy's message meant; then the little woman covered her face, and refusing to be comforted continually moaned:

"Oh, Joe! My brave darling! I wounded your love, and now you will never come back to me."

Judge Mabry loaned his dead son's friend money enough to purchase suitable clothing and pay his fare back to his old home, where he went, and for more than two years there was no word from him until one day there came from the post-office a letter directed in a bold, angular and decidedly peculiar hand, and bearing a strange North Carolina post-mark. Tom was at home from College, it being vacation, and we may well imagine that the entire family listened with rare pleasure to the following rambling epistle from their old friend:

" JOETOWN, NORTH CAROLINA,
"August 16th, 1867.

" *Dear Judge* : I know you all will be pleased to hear from me and I have no excuse for not writing earlier except a desire to surprise you pleasantly. Well, I came home directly from your house and found Susan looking prettier and sweeter than ever. You may imagine I didn't take any excuse but went to see the parson and in one week we were married. I am still the happiest man in 'Ole North Carliney,' and I still don't care who knows it. Well, sir, as soon as we were married she took hold of me and said that whilst I was good enough for her, or anybody else, yet for my own sake she proposed to put an extra polish on me. Would you believe it, sir? She got some books and put me regularly at school. She was the teacher and it would have made a horse laugh to hear me spell. Of course I

knew a little about spelling—mostly the phonetic style,
as Susan called it, but she made me buckle to and learn.
It was well she took hold of me in time, for when I got
well used to her I was so interested in my studies that
a regiment of cavalry couldn't have stopped me. I
have learned about all that Susan can teach me—and
her father was sensible enough to give her a fair education for this backwoods country—so you see I am a
long ways in advance of my educational condition of
two years ago. I reckon I am still what poor dear, Joe,
used to call 'a rough diamond,' but Susan has polished
me somewhat.

"In the mean time I had to work very hard, but there
was an excellent valley on Susan's place, and I made
good crops, so what with plenty of deer in the mountains and trout in the river we never suffered for pro-
visions.

"This would seem to be enough good fortune for a
poor devil like me, but there was more luck in the pot
for me, and I couldn't keep my hands away from it.
A poor little hundred-acre farm that was my boyhood
home was still mine, but there was no good soil on it,
and as it joined Susan's place I used it for a hog pasture—there being a world of mast on it in the fall.
About one year ago a man from Pennsylvania—that
place with the long name, that riled me so the first
time we met—came here and examined the hills for
several days. He stayed at my house, and I noticed
that he wandered about my hog-pasture so much that
I began to suspect him of designs upon my shoats, so

I 'upt' and asked him what he was after. He said he liked the country, and if I would take five hundred dollars for that little tract it was a bargain. Now I had heard of five hundred such bargains, so I looked him right square in the face and told him that the land was worth more to me than it possibly could be to him—seeing that he didn't have any hogs to feed— and that if he had discovered anything of value about the place I would do the fair thing for the information. You see I began to smell a gold mine at once, but he told me that there was enough granite of fine quality, and easy of access, in that old hill where I sat that night when the devil was wrestling with me about Pete Brownlow, to build a city, and that he was authorized to offer me twenty thousand dollars for the property.

" When I heard that sum of money named I like to have fainted, but I told him I would answer him in half an hour. You see I wanted to talk with Susan about it and get her opinion, for you must know that I still cling to my old assertion that 'there never wus sech a gal as Susan.' After we talked it over I told the man that if the property was worth twenty thousand dollars a half interest ought to be worth ten thousand, and that I would rather not sell the whole thing. He finally told me that they would give me the ten thousand in cash and ten thousand in non-assessable stock, besides making me the vice-president of the company.

" That big title settled me, so now I have the money and am a vice-president. We have two hundred men at work, have run a tap of the railroad up to the quarry, have built a town, established a post-office, and are doing a hog-killing business. We keep up such a row all the time with giant cartridges that I have to go ten miles off to find a deer, and I sometimes dream that I am back in Petersburg.

"They wanted to call the town Knighton, but I stuck out for 'Joetown,' and so it is. I have just been elected to the Legislature from this county, and must spend a part of my time trying to get used to the city ways and airs of Raleigh. The other fellow said that he could prove that I stole a horse when I lived in Louisiana, but when I told him that unless he did prove it I would make him eat a peck of dirt at one meal he ''lowed' he was joking. He didn't carry the joke any further.

"Well, my dear Judge, I have written a long letter, for me, and now I must close. My regards to Major Carter and Colonel DuPree, and if you ever see John Barton tell him I have quit the furniture-breaking business. Please remember me to all my old friends, to whom I shall always feel grateful for so many acts of kindness received while in your midst. God bless you!

"With much love for you and yours, I am your grateful friend,   CALEB KNIGHT, V. P.

"P. S.—There is the finest boy in old North Carolina at our house, and we call him Joseph Mabry Knight."

*   *   *   *   *   *   *

On the third anniversary of Joe's death a carriage containing a lady and two gentlemen drove out from Petersburg. One of the gentlemen was a tall, boyish-looking young man about nineteen years of age; the other was a person of gigantic frame, and kindly face nearly hidden under a heavy brown beard, both hair and beard more streaked with white than his age would justify. Their companion was dressed in black, and her fair face showed traces of sorrow, but no tears had ever been able to quench the brightness of those eyes, that had in years gone by looked down into the soul of the poor soldier boy and made him a captive forever.

When the carriage stopped at the grass-grown line of earthworks the occupants alighted, and the elder gentleman acting as guide, they climbed into the fortifications.

"Here," said Goodnight, "is the place where we passed out of our works, and just by that little clump of oaks your brother led his regiment. Just there, Tom, the alarm was given, and as we mounted that little rise the first load of grape and canister passed over our heads. The next shot piled up some gallant fellows, and the third would have done a power of mischief if Joe hadn't been so quick and stopped the fellow who was fixing the lanyard. This is the way we went, and there in front of us are the walls of Fort Steadman, where so many of our brave men lost their lives."

Jennie shuddered as she looked upon those mute mementoes of the great struggle, and Tom's heart swelled within him as he thought of the heroic boy

who climbed over those walls amid the storm of battle.
When they reached the fort Goodnight helped Jennie
across the ditch and upon the walls.

"Here is the place we mounted," said he, "and right
across this point young Featherstone, Joe's friend, was
lying with a bullet in his heart. See this little flat
cove of a place with the rotting timbers! Here was
the big cannon, and under it I sat down with Joe in
my arms, taking no more interest in the battle than if
I had been a thousand miles away. It makes me right
weak now to think about it."

Jennie's fortitude had sustained her admirably up to
this point, but here she broke down and the sweet little
woman wept as if it were but yesterday that her lover
died. Tom tried to be a man and keep back the great
lump that was in his throat, but the poor fellow utterly
failed, and, going aside to a little mound, sat down and
wiped away the blessed tears that came direct from his
soft, boyish heart. No shame upon him that he should
weep, but rather shame upon the man whose heart-
fountains are dried and whose tenderest feelings have
been allowed to wither.

After awhile they passed on to the graves under the
tree, and there beneath that mighty pine they lingered
until the western sky flushed red about the setting sun.
Then, as the whippoorwill in a neighboring thicket
struck up his evening song, the fair girl took leave of
her dead lover and went slowly away through the twilight to begin another volume of life, in which Joe
will only be known as a holy memory!

And here we, too, must leave one of our heroes to sleep with the "noble army of martyrs," taking this comfort in our sorrow—the tenderest love and the sublimest patriotism of all the coming years will cluster about that lowly grave, and all heroic endeavor will emulate the dead defender of a vanished nation. We leave you now, dear Joe ; but the young men and maidens will strew your grave with flowers at every return of spring, and by the hearthstone on many a winter night the old soldier will tell to wondering little ones the story of your death.

CHAPTER XVII.

TOM THE PLOUGHMAN AND BURNS THE POET.

WHEN all armed resistance to the Federal authority ceased the people of the South had reason to dread the return of civil authority. The magnanimous terms proposed by General Grant at the surrender were regarded with wonder, but they knew that with the end of the war would come the end of that remarkable man's power; that when the army was disbanded and the fierce warriors of the hustings garrisoned every courthouse all over the land, there would come such a time of proscription and petty-wrongs as never before humiliated a brave people. They were not mistaken. True it is, there were but few imprisonments, and no executions directly on account of the war, nor were the terms of the military surrender violated, but a policy was adopted in settling the political affairs of the seceded States that for ten years after hostilities ceased engendered feelings more antagonistic than those made alive in actual conflict.

We will not discuss the policy of Reconstruction, for in the light of history it proved a mournful failure. We may forget the horrors of the war when we remember its glory, but the insults of after days will never be forgotten. The people of the South absolutely refused to be comforted by such a return into the Union, and would not be reconstructed. They turned their attention to the great problem of making a living under the new order of things, and left political matters to their former slaves, who were marshaled by as conscience-less a set of plunderers as ever held office. They did not willingly or carelessly neglect public affairs, but such a vast number were disfranchised that the remainder would not engage in a controversy that was as hopeless as it was nauseating—besides, while unarmed and helpless, they would not engage in a struggle with armed men. They thought the war had ended with the surrender of the armies, but soon found out their mistake. It was hard enough to remain at home in sullen indifference and eschew politics, but when reckless financial management, rightfully called stealing, had destroyed the last vestige of State credit, and no more bonds could be sold at even the most ruinous discount, the spoilers reached out after the property of the people with a rate of taxation and assessment that was equivalent to confiscation. The people stood all the exactions and arbitrary thefts of certain bureau officials, but when affairs culminated in bankruptcy, there was another "rebellion." The first, so-called, was in favor of "States rights," the last was for individual rights. The former was for a political theory; the latter for preservation of homes, for wives and little ones. It was bound to succeed. No array of bayonets nor the thunder of cannon can coerce a people defending their homes. The people of the North did not comprehend

the condition of affairs in the South. They do not now.
They had acquiesced in a policy adopted by their leaders and took no further interest in the matter—except
that for years they heedlessly endorsed every act of the
party in power, without inquiring into its justice.

Not ten days would the people of Pennsylvania have
endured such outrages as were the common lot of the
property owners in Louisiana for years. The fires of
rebellion would have glowed from the Delaware to the
Alleghany until the curse was removed, and the western mountains would have trembled under the thunders of outraged liberty. Yet, it is a fact that for more
than ten years the people of the latter State suffered
and waited, however impatiently, for the mailed hand
to be taken from their throats—all the while being assured that the war had ended. Under the stress of a
new public opinion North, the heavy military hand
was removed, and as the temporal power of Rome
passed away with French bayonets, so the robber rule
ended in Louisiana, when the last blue coat filed out
of the State-house, leaving the people to republican liberty and the management of their own affairs. Once
in a while some candid business man from one of the
great cities would visit the South and with keen perception would note the wretched state of affairs, then
upon his return home he would tell with indignation
the story of the wrongs endured by that people until
the generous sense of a great nation was aroused, and
they saw with dismay that in emancipating and enfran-
chising the slave they had enslaved the master. The

American people are primarily just in their ideas and estimate of things, but in the mad struggle for business they sometimes forget the claims of justice—yet not long.   The heart and brain of the individual as well as of the nation are in the closest sympathy, and generally we find the most careful judgment hand in hand with the warmest sentiment.

We mention this condition of affairs because it affects the fortunes of some of our characters, and is far reaching in its influences upon their lives.

In the midst of these political troubles Tom went away to college, and years passed before he realized the patient labor and loving sacrifices of his good old father that enabled him to remain.   We think had he done so earlier he would have employed his time to better purpose.   He would have studied harder and thought less of frolicking.   No doubt he would have promenaded fewer times under the oaks in front of the "Gallery," a name bestowed by the students upon a certain young ladies' academy in the same village. Instead of tinkling his guitar and catching cold to the tune of the "Lone Starry Hours" in front of that same academy, he would have excelled in his classes.   He would have been satisfied with one-half the number of gorgeous neckties and high-heeled boots.   Perhaps— but the very doubt implies an extra doubt—he would have fallen in love fewer times and would have been able to translate his Greek Testament lesson on Monday morning without the assistance of King James and his host of divines.

To become a thorough student a boy must not be in love. The harassing doubts and uncertain hopes that come between him and his lessons are not conducive to study, and he dreams away the hours that ought to be devoted to better purpose. He should ignore Cupid, and bow only at the shrine of knowledge. Give him more of Cicero and less of Ovid. Teach him how to become a man. He will become a lover without any teaching.

It was Irving who told of the young prince who had been brought up in seclusion, so that he had never seen a woman. Unfortunately for the peace of his realm, while out walking one day he met three girls, daintily arrayed, and boy-like, took an intense interest in them at once. His guardian, whom it is needless to add, was old and ugly, hurried him away, telling him that those creatures he saw were devils such as vex and undo mankind; but ever as the poor fellow wearied of his studies he would heave a deep sigh and exclaim: "Oh, that little devil in blue!" We are told that his passion brought him unnumbered woes, and cost him his kingdom.

To the average college boy the "little devil in blue" is too often present, enticing him away from his books and filling his mind with idle fancies or his heart with foolish dreams. From what we can learn of Tom there is every reason to suppose that bright little devils in every hue of the rainbow disturbed his boyish heart and danced with fairy feet over every page from Xenophon to Differential Calculus. If he essayed to study

botany the fair, laughing face of Madge looked out
from its pages amidst a shower of rose-petals, and even
among the Evidences of Christianity he saw the pew
of Major Carter in the old hill-country church, while
the Sunday morning odor of violets came stealing o'er
his senses.   No study was so dry and no problem so
abstruse but some bright-eyed Gertrude or blushing
Kate peeped over the top of the page and won for him
a dreamy demerit.   Even amid the clouds of algebraic
dust that ever surrounds the unknown "X" he saw the
brown ringlets and the little dimpled hands that waved
welcome to the great steamer so long ago.   It would
have been well for Tom had he called up his great
will-power and banished those bright fancies, but he
went on dreaming until the day came that he must
meet the world in the supreme struggle for place.
Then he saw how idle were those dreams, and how
unfitted he was for the work allotted him.   Poor fellow!   His heart ached many a time when for appearance sake he must be cheerful; but it was a brave heart
and hopeful, so he worked with an energy that atoned
somewhat for time lost in dreaming—and dreamed
again at odd moments.   His heart was tenderer for
those lost dreams, and maybe that will count for something in the final reckoning.

The sad condition of the country had its effect upon
Judge Mabry's fortunes, and little by little, under the
new system of labor, the burden of taxation, and depre-
ciation of values, the remnant of his wealth disappeared.   He was growing older in strength than in

years, and when his noble form stooped he missed the strong arm of the brave boy who slept beneath the old pine in front of Petersburg. The most common of all the pitiable sights in the Southland since the war is the aged father or mother tottering on to the grave, calling vainly for the dead boy who sleeps upon some distant battle-field! As the Judge grew older he became, if possible, gentler. The peace which flowed like a river through his heart was such as comes down to the weary soul that hears the voice of the Master, and the light that shone upon his face came not from material sun nor stars.

One day Tom came home and went to work. He saw the wreck, and rolling up his sleeves he seized hold of the plow-handles with an energy born of prospective want.

The poet Burns was a ploughman, and so was Tom. Nor are we afraid to suggest that he could discount the poet in cutting correct furrows, even as the poet could excel Tom in penning divine verse—and it is a fact that the latter used to woo the muse sometimes, in a quiet way. If, however, a tiny mouse ran from under his plow he did not pause to sing its funeral, but killed it in a natural way and went on turning the sod. If the lark sprang up at his feet and filled the air with melody as it soared towards the sky, he thought unutterable things and sighed for his shotgun when he remembered that the musical little wretch was a "terror" among the young corn. Tom never stayed out on Saturday night with jolly companions, singing doubtful songs and drinking bad beer in some ale-house, but slept the healthy sleep of the granger, and went to church next morning in the vain hope that Madge would not observe his sunburnt hands and blistered nose.   We think, if we may judge from the conduct of the two ploughmen, that our Tom was the better man.   Yet when he has gone to his reward and the old hills he used to plough have gone with the waters into the valley; when he and Madge, with all they knew or loved, shall have been forgotten—yea, when the very species of corn that Tom used to plant shall have been lost to agriculture, the poet with his sweet songs of the daisy and the mouse—also of the little creature that rhymes with mouse—will be fresh in a world's memory.   This is manifestly unjust, but we shall not attempt to correct it, nor shall we try to explain why our young man was not considered quite so nice as when his hands were white and his head a shade softer.

Personally a man who follows the plough is not so acceptable in society although mentally and morally he may outrank most of his fellows.   There is an indefinable air of horse lots and newly-ploughed soil in his manner that clings to him, even in the ball-room.   He may be fit to command armies and do deeds of daring or kindness that make him immortal, but society has another standard to which the poor ploughman may never hope to reach.   People go into raptures over the performance of a great English statesman who once or twice during the year pulls off his coat and chops down a British oak, and they even carry away the chips as so many priceless souvenirs for the admiration of a hero-worshiping world, but suppose that noble old Englishman was compelled to cut wood for a living? Suppose!

The drawing-room does not always look to a man's moral worth.

Tom was a great admirer of the ploughman Burns, and thought the poet must have directed the most of his sweetest verses to the great-grandmother of Madge, so well did they. sing the loveliness of the daughter. He was always ready at less than a moment's notice to rhapsodize that maiden's charms in tenderest verse. Three years absence at college had wrought wonders in Tom, and his little princess had donned the airs and skirts of a young lady, so the old-time intimacy was gone, and stately formalism took the place of innocent confidence.

Madge was the very spirit of life and mirth, but she exhibited in Tom's presence a reserve that he was not wise enough to understand; so he grew savage under the torture, and resented what he took to be indifference. One day he sought her, and with stammering tongue told her how her coldness wounded him, and how he had always loved her since they were children together.

"You are cruel to me, Madge," said he; "you can be as full of life as a bird when you are with others, yet when I try to talk to you I am answered with 'yes' and 'no.'"

"I don't see why you should say so, I am sure," replied Madge hotly. "If I am livelier with others maybe it is because they try better to entertain me. You are accusing me wrongfully."

"It looks that way to me, Madge; and I don't understand it. I know that I am poor and have to work hard for a living; but I try to do my duty, and you will never find a man who will love you more earnestly and unselfishly."

"I thank you for the love, Tom, which I am sure is honest, and I am unworthy of it, but you are foolishly unjust. Besides, I am not hunting for a man of any sort; and your remark about poverty is entirely out of place. It is a mean insinuation that I care for wealth rather than love, and is unworthy of you."

Then the young lady got angry, and the more Tom tried to explain the more foolish things he said and the angrier she became, until finally she told him that he had better remain away until he formed a more correct opinion of one he professed to love.

Tom was very simple in those days, and just then he acted very foolishly. Instead of going away and letting the storm blow over he undertook to argue the matter. When he grew older he learned how useless it was to argue with a woman; especially an angry woman. When he left he said:

"Good-bye, Madge! When you think you will be glad to see me say so, and I'll come to you though I have to cross the seas."

"If you wait until I send for you I think you'll grow tired," was the reply of that spirited young lady, with just a suspicion of slang. And thus they parted.

As a result of this quarrel Tom went home swelling with wrath; and Madge, like a true woman, went to her room and indulged in a good cry.

"Poor, dear Tom!" she said to her confidential pillow that night—"he is awfully foolish sometimes, but he is just as brave and generous as he can be. I was ugly to him this evening, but, never mind, it will be all right when we meet again."

When she went off to sleep she dreamed that a great river separated her from her lover, and while they followed down its banks beckoning and calling to each other the stream grew wider and wider, until she could hear his voice no more.

Tom experienced a change of heart also, that night, and mentally kicked himself a dozen times for being an idiot.

"Bless her little heart! I was a fool, and I am afraid it has become a fixed habit with me, that I must try to break myself of. She's spirited, and I love her all the more for it. When I see her again I'll own up what a booby I was, and I'll bet a thousand dollars she'll forgive me." Then he went to sleep, too, and his dreams were such awful things as visit the pillow of a man who has eaten too much supper.

Tom quit betting such ponderous sums of money after that, and confined himself to such society stakes as a pair of gloves or a pound of bonbons.

The next day Madge went away to school, and when in after years they met again both she and Tom were as much wiser as they were older.

CHAPTER XVIII.

TOM worked very hard during two crop seasons; then one day when he had ploughed to the end of a long row that was ambushed every yard with stumps and roots he swore mildly and went to the house.

"Mother!"—he exclaimed. "I'm going to quit ploughing. It don't pay, and, besides, if I follow that mule another week they'll have to turn me out of the church."

This was very wicked in Tom, but, dear reader, if you never ploughed with a mule in fallow ground where vines and roots and various other diabolical agencies lie in wait to harrow up your very soul; or, if you never drove a team of oxen during a hot day over a rough road, and wrestled with them in a miry pool of water, you are unacquainted with even the rudiments of vexation. A ninety days' note going to protest, or the loss of an election where your money has gone like water for "legitimate campaign expenses," is an innocent amusement in comparison. The man who can plough over a two-acre patch of such ground and not lapse into profanity is a slow milk-and-water chap who wouldn't swear any how, or he is in daily expectation of a pair of wings.

Of course it is wrong to swear, and any man who uses profane language, no matter under what provication, is not altogether the nice gentleman that he was before. His moral perception is to a certain degree blunted, and his soul is not so fair as it was. The most overwhelming evil in polite society to-day is the profane tendency of conversation among gentlemen, and it would be bad enough if they used only strong expletives without coupling therewith the sacred Name, but the sacrilege is, unfortunately, always present.

"And mother," continued Tom, "I am afraid I swore a little when the plough handle punched me in the ribs and I struck my shin against the hard end of a root."

"Oh, Tom! Are you not ashamed of yourself? How badly your dear father would feel if he heard of your using profane language! You had better get some soap and wash your mouth as I used to make you do when you said ugly words. Then, my dear son, there is a stain on your pure soul that no soap and water will wash away."

"I know it was naughty, mammy dear; but have'nt I confessed? What's the good of confession if you are not forgiven? Besides I didn't swear very bad; not much worse than the poor little 'dog-gone' I used to use when a little boy. I won't do so any more unless I go back to the plough, in which event I won't make any rash promises."

We are glad to record that our young man quit swearing—when he quit ploughing.

The good old Judge grew feebler and more uncom-
plaining as the weeks passed, and one day the old man,
who had always been so active, remained seated by the
fire.   He did not stir out that day, nor the next, and
soon it came about that his easy chair was placed for
him in vain; but he remained in bed, and the good
mother busied herself to prepare little appetizing
dishes for him, which were often untouched.   Sometimes one or another of the family read to him a sweet
Psalm, or those ever-soothing words: "Let not your
hearts be troubled."   He talked often of Joe in those
days, and told little incidents of the young soldier's
childhood that had escaped the memory of busier people.   He did not seem to regard his boy as dead, but
only absent, and that one day he would return.   The
family humored all his conceits, and lingered about
his bed with the tenderest solicitude, always seeking
to anticipate his wants.   The weeks lengthened into
months, and the glad Christmas time was brightening
o'er all the earth when it became apparent that the
busy life was about to be surrendered.   The evening
sun was low down the western sky on the day before
Christmas, and all the family were about the bedside,
when the sick man aroused, and looking around on
the different faces, asked:

"Where is Joe?"

"He will be here directly, dear," answered the mother
as her kind eyes filled with tears.

"Open the window, please?   I want to see the sky."
The sufferer looked long and lovingly out over the
10

yard and across the expanse of field stretching away
to the swamp where our Tom found shelter during the
last day of the war, then there stole over his face an
expression of abundant peace. What were his thoughts
in that solemn hour angels may never tell, but we
know that they were pure and holy.

"Ah, yes! that will do, thank you. How glorious
is the sun in his setting. 'The heavens declare the
glory of God,'" then with a sigh of comfort he sank
back on his pillow saying:

"Now let me rest," and the everlasting gates opened
wide for the faithful old man.

"Oh, kindest of fathers and bravest of brothers!"
exclaimed Tom weeping. "You have left me desolate, and the earth is poorer since you went away."

The night after the funeral of Judge Mabry only
Tom, his sister Janet, and mother were left of the disconsolate family, and these were seated about a great
fire in the old parlor. The others had homes of their
own, with new ties and new duties.

"Mother," said Tom after a pause, "this is no country for me. I do not think that I can make a living out
of these old hills, and I have determined to go away
to some section where there is a chance for a young
man. I think I shall seek some place to put my
knowledge of civil engineering into practice, and I am
informed that in the great Northwest there is no end
to railroad building, tunneling and bridging. Here I
can do nothing, with the terrible curse hanging over
our State. There is absolutely nothing to do except

digging in the soil, and I am tired of that. I have no means to go into planting extensively, and I would likely loose all I have any way with this poor system of labor. The condition of affairs here is bound to end sooner or later if we have to fight over it again, and as certain as fate there will be more blood letting all over this Southland. I am going away, but if this people get into a row with the scalawags and negroes I will return and give dear old Joe's sword some fresh work to do. I am glad that clever Yankee officer sent it home, and I should like to know him for I feel sure I would like him. Some men have big souls. But regarding these internal troubles, and the unbearable insolence of the negroes, I speak but the sentiments of our entire people, who have no desire to try the issue of another war, but will not be dogged to death by a parcel of money-seeking reprobates from the North."

Tom was but a boy, yet he spoke the sentiments of men. It is a fact that five years after the close of the late war the people of the South, under what was termed "carpet-bag rule," were in more of a fighting humor than at any time during the conflict, and but for wiser counsels both North and South the internal troubles South would have burst forth into actual war. There were more than a million desperate men whose reckless fury would have caused more loss of blood and treasure than the world ever saw in one struggle. It would not have been a war of brothers, but the un-tamed wrath of blood-thirsty tigers. The people of the South were desperate, and they were united as they

never were before. Men who would not fight for a
political idea, or a social theory, would have gone to
death under personal wrong, and the solemn, immuta-
ble truth remains that a race of Anglo-Saxon masters
will never rest under the domination of their late
slaves—nor, in fact, under any other tyranny. It took
the people of the North a long while to find this out,
and they would only believe it after thousands of their
old soldiers had come here to live, and had become
imbued with the same spirit of resistance. They were
slow to learn that brute force would never solve the
Southern question. Their citizens came here to live—
strong, active, energetic fellows, and the first lesson
they learned was that the white man must rule. Never
did school have pupils more apt. So it came about
that better ideas prevailed, and to-day, except when
some old political hack wants an office or some idiot
needs confinement, a stranger would never know there
had been a war. The same feelings expressed by Tom
actuated every man, and the same hope of finding a
land where race troubles were unknown and there was
a prospect of reward for energy and industry, drove
thousands of our best people away. Many went to
Texas or California, and many more, like our Tom,
determined to go to the Yankee and learn his ways.

Thus it happened that when the sun of a bright
"New Year" broke through the fog that hung in great
clouds over the mighty Mississippi its first rays fell
upon the deck of an up-country steamer and lighted
up the sad features of a tall young man who had

started out into the world in search of fortune, and had left Belhaven forever. Away from the grave of father; away from the scenes forever hallowed by the memory of Joe; away from the presence of Madge, and into the untried realities of life among strangers went Tom, so no wonder that when at night he lay in his little cabin listening to the ponderous strokes of the great engine, and heard the rush of dark waters, a feeling of utter loneliness came over him and there was the moisture of tears upon his pillow.

From St. Louis he wrote a letter to mother telling her that he would start the next morning out to the mountains of the West, where he hoped to find work and build a new home among that bustling people. That night ere he retired he penned a short note to his little Princess. He wrote:

"Madge, dear, you were angry with me when we parted, but there were tears in your sweet eyes, so I think I may yet hope. I have gone away out of your life, and away from all I love, yet some day I trust to see you again. You told me to leave you, and I have done so. When you call me back I will come. I shall listen ever for your call. You know my heart, and you can trust me. Good-bye.

"Your faithful

"Tom."

Such was the little missive that sweet Madge wept over and read again and again for many a year, until its words were burned into her heart.

The next morning, away past bustling new cities, through vast fields of young grain, over mighty rivers and through dark tunnels, away he whirled past lonely farm-houses and restless herds of cattle; away, on and on, over plains of sand where the cayote skulked amid the sage-brush, until one bright afternoon Tom looked out and for the first time beheld the snow-capped mountains towering towards the heavens.

Those western mountains have taken into their shadows the adventurous youth of every State. Some come out strong and fair, while others wreck their young manhood and are forever lost to waiting loved ones. Tom had but a few dollars left and he had no intention of loitering. His first thought was to secure work. Several of the great railroads were pushing out into the mountain country, and to effect their purposes required an enormous outlay of muscle, money and skill. No young man with a will to work need be idle. There was plenty to do if one was not too particular. Arriving at Denver, the wonderful young mountain city, Tom enjoyed a good night's rest, and then bright and early he sought the office of the W. Y. Railway, where he was in waiting long before the officials were in their places. He walked the corridor impatiently until he was accosted by a kindly old gentleman with—

"Well, my young man, what can we do for you to-day?"

"If you please," replied Tom, "I would be glad to see Col. Elmore, the Chief Engineer. Is he in?"

"Yes, you are fortunate in finding him here. Had you been an hour later you would have been compelled to seek him a hundred miles away in the mountains. Come this way"—and following as he was directed, he was ushered into the presence of a fine, soldierly looking man with brown beard and mustache.

"Colonel Elmore," spoke the old gentleman, "here is a young man who seeks you early and looks like he means business."

"Be seated sir," said Colonel Elmore, courteously, "and tell me what I can do for you."

"You are very kind sir," answered Tom. "My name is Thomas Mabry, and I am hunting for work. I have studied civil engineering and am anxious to become practically expert in that line, but I am ready to do any honorable work you may give me."

Tom was trembling with excitement by this time, for it was his first venture out into the world and he greatly feared a denial. Colonel Elmore, smiled in sympathy for the stammering fellow, and came to his rescue by saying:

"You look like an honest, courageous young man, and I think we can find something for you to do. Where are you from?"

"I hope, sir, you won't let it militate against me," answered Tom, "but I am from the far South—from Louisiana." Tom had spoken indiscreetly, as he often did, and was thunderstruck at the answer. He should have simply stated his residence, and raised no question of prejudice.

"We don't want any rebels here," said the Colonel, sternly, "and unless you have left your treasonable sentiments behind you had better go back to your own section. You Louisiana rebels are giving the government a world of trouble any how and should be dealt with severely."

If Tom had been foolish in his answer he now showed the grand courage of his convictions, and springing to his feet with blazing face and fierce words he replied—

"I have always heard that you cussed Yankees were a malignant, unforgiving set, with no good word or deed for a man who does not agree with you. I spurn your offer of work, sir, and I will gladly go back to where people have souls. Leave my sentiments behind! I'll speak them anywhere on God's footstool that it pleases me to open my mouth. I am ashamed of you, Colonel Elmore! And to think that you claim to be an American—oh, I'm disappointed in you! When I was so pleased with your reception and your looks. Colonel Elmore, you look like a gentleman, but—God help me!—you don't act like one. I'll go, sir; but I would advise you to come South and learn how to be a gentleman."

Colonel Elmore broke out into a ringing laugh at this last remark, and said:

"Hold on, my boy! I was only trying you to see if you would stand up for your side. I am satisfied Sit down again and let me tell you my views Don't misjudge me. Louisiana is an American State, and her sons are my brothers. I am a New Yorker, but I may become a Georgian, or a Texan, or a citizen of any other State to-morrow; yet first, last and all the time I am an American! I think I shall be proud of you, and if you are the metal I take you to be you will find no trouble about employment. It will rest with you whether or not you succeed. Come now and let us 'shake hands across the bloody chasm,' until we can get out to the front, when we will fill it up with dirt and rocks!"

"And your name is Mabry? Do you know a Judge Mabry, of Louisiana? He lives in Feliciana parish."

At the mention of that name Tom's eyes filled with tears, and he replied:

"He was my father. One of the best and dearest of men."

"*Was* your father? I am truly sorry to know that he is dead. I have a letter from him written some years ago in answer to a note from me when I sent him the sword of his gallant son, who was killed just as he had captured my gun at Fort Steadman. It is a noble letter; so dignified and kindly in tone, and so full of gratitude to me for sending home his boy's sword. I am truly glad to meet you, Tom; I won't stand on ceremony with you; and you shall have pleasant employment, as much for the sake of your noble old father and your heroic brother, as for your own. Get yourself ready to go with me to the front, where your place will be in the future. I will start in an hour. Pack your valise, and you can store your trunk in our warehouse until you make permanent arrangements."

"Colonel Elmore!" exclaimed the happy boy, "I don't know how to thank you in words, but I will prove to you that I am grateful when I go to work in your employ. I want to beg your pardon, too, for the hard things I said about the Yankees, for I am sure now that they are not all mean."

"No more of that, my boy. The better you know our people the more you will admire them, and this will teach you a lesson. Never condemn any person or nationality upon hearsay. Most persons have some good in them. Let us get to work now."

Promptly at the hour the chief engineer's car rolled out upon its journey to the construction camp, and our Tom was a passenger. It was his first ride among the mountains, and Colonel Elmore, seeing how absorbed the boy was in the grand panorama which moved swiftly past him, did not disturb him save to call his attention to some especially beautiful view.

"This is vastly different from my Louisiana home, Colonel, and I confess it attracts me with its beauty and novelty. There I walk out amid the grand old forest trees and when I view the heavens I must look up, so they seem a great way off; but here from these elevations I look away and see the sky coming down all around me until it grasps the earth in its embrace, or when we rush into some deep valley it seems further off than ever."

"To me," responded Colonel Elmore, "these glorious hills are forever new. I love the mountains as I love nothing else in nature, and I think I shall make my home among them some day. There is such variety about the mountains that one never tires. One hour they are clothed in happy sunshine, yet in the next the soft white mists will cling about them like the garments of a bride. To-day the peace of Heaven seems to rest upon them, but to-morrow they will tremble amid the thunders of some unchained tempest. Yes, I love the mountains, although one would think, from the tunnels I bore and the great gaps I cut through them, that they were a line of mortal enemies I am bound to destroy."

Our party soon reached the terminus of the road, and here Tom saw one of those peripatetic towns of which the people of old settled communities can have no conception—a town that drops itself with a rattle and bang into some quiet valley to-day, and for a month or more seems all the time one motley circus performance, then moves on, leaving the once lovely spot to desolation and abandoned tin cans. There are also a half score or more of lonely graves, where rest the bodies of men who "died with their boots on," or women who sought forgetfulness in the deadly opium. The host of gamblers, laborers, loafers, and courtesans have moved on to make a six-weeks' hell in some other quiet spot.

Tom went to work at once. His kind new friend showed him what he wanted done and how, then the old energy of the cotton farm blazed up under the impetus of a great purpose—to win for himself a name and his dear ones a home. He was fortunate in the friendship of Colonel Elmore, and there was no reason why the handsome soldier of thirty years of age and the grave youth of twenty should not become intimate, being congenial spirits amid a crowd of earth's roughest sons.

Day after day and week after week the explosion of giant cartridges reminded them of the stormy days then gone, and under those batteries of peace the great rocks of the mountain side yielded and went thundering into the gorges far below. Brain and muscle worked on, until through dark tunnels and mighty cuts, over massive culverts and airy bridges, the car of latter-day progress went booming into wilds known only to the trapper, the hunter, and the miner. Tom worked and never seemed to tire. He was in his element, driving and pushing like the progress of an age depended upon his individual exertion, nor did he neglect to save his earnings.

When the icy arms of winter grasped all the mountains and reared among them snowy palaces whose beauty lured adventurous men to death, he went back to Denver, and in his chief's office he wrought mechanical problems of such apparent value, and gave such careful attention to all the details of business, that when the spring campaign opened the authorities took notice of him and he was appointed First Assistant to the Chief Engineer, with great authority in the construction department.

CHAPTER XIX.

"GOD PITY THEM BOTH AND PITY US ALL."

NOT far from the pretty little mountain town of Quimby, on this new road, there is a valley of surpassing loveliness, and its beauty is not its only merit—for it was its fertility that attracted our Tom's agricultural eye. It was a portion of the Government grant to the railroad, and to see it was to want it; so he hastened to headquarters and put in a bid for it. A few days later he was as proud over his "quarter section" as ever a young father was over his first-born son. He walked up and down the valley, stopped to admire every clump of trees, dropped pebbles into every trout-hole along the little brook, and climbed the hills on either side to become familiar with every view of his possessions. No lover ever went out of his path to view his sweetheart's home oftener than Tom held his train, just a few minutes, until he could run to a neighboring hill and look over into his valley.

Three months later dear old Belhaven had passed into the hands of strangers, and mother with the fair sister Janet had come to dwell in the cosiest of cottages, which Tom had built among the hemlocks and box-alders where the little trout-stream broke out from the hills. Here they lived in peace, and the old home

(229)

became a tender dream such as brings back our childhood to mellow old age. Here on the afternoons of Saturdays Tom would come home from his work in front and rest from his labors. On the Sabbath they would climb the hill to where the village chapel attracted those devoutly inclined, and within its sacred walls they almost forgot that the old hill-country church of Feliciana was waiting in vain for their coming. All during that glorious summer and autumn life seemed like a foretaste of something happier than this world can offer. Sometimes Colonel Elmore would stop his train at Quimby and walk down to the cottage with Tom to enjoy a social tea with the family, and here it was that the fair, blushing Janet poured the hot tea so daintily that it warmed his bachelor heart. Tom used to wonder why the brave Colonel took such pleasure in stopping át their little home so often. He thought that it was the wonderful biscuit that his mother used to make, and was confirmed in that belief when he saw his friend put away a half dozen of them at a sitting.

"Good heavens!" thought Tom, "if we only had some of those delicious old Louisiana yams, and mother would make such a potato pone as she used to cook for father, the Colonel would want to board with us. No wonder he eats so, after a week of such fare as we have in front."

Tom loved to see his friend eat, and when after each cake he laughed over some funny story he was sorry there was a limit to the man's appetite. The days fled swiftly, and our young man was happy as youth, hope, health and employment can insure; but let us not suppose for a moment that he had forgotten his little Princess. Ah, no! That beautiful valley was selected, and the pretty cottage built, with a hope that one day Madge would look with the approval of loving eyes upon his work, and brighten with her presence a home that would soften his sorrow for the lost Belhaven. Poor foolish, faithful Tom!

And what of the pretty Madge during those years? She went to school during nine months of the year, and the other three months were to her so many seasons of triumph. She had finally gone off for a term to a finishing school in Virginia, and was now preparing to be turned loose upon the world. Happy world, so soon to be at the feet of such loveliness!

One July day when the little town of Quimby never looked so fair there came a letter for Tom, in a square womanly envelope, and directed in the tiniest of feminine characters. He saw it and blushed lest the postmaster should notice his confusion. Had there been a postmistress the secret would have been guessed in a moment, but the obtuse person in charge never saw anything unusual, and only remarked:

"How careless these young men are! Here's that chap gone off without his change, and fifty cents is added to my salary."

What did Tom care for fifty cents? He had something that the President could not buy, and he felt rich. He walked away down the hill; or rather he floated down, for every step was upon springs, and his heart was so light it almost bore him up. If he touched anything so material as the earth he was not then aware of it. Sitting down in the pleasant shade upon a great table-rock that jutted out from the hillside, he drew the precious missive from his pocket, and for several blissful minutes studied the pretty little characters that made up the address. Who ever put such a dear little curved tail to a "T" save Madge? and the roundest little "o" that ever ravished a lover's eye. Did anybody ever see such a perfect "m" since the days of Cadmus? Never! The capital "M" was a poem, while those exquisite little letters "a, b, r, y" were such things as fairies dream of in the time of apple blossoms. The "Esq" which rounded the address into perfect symmetry was the only real abbreviation of the title that ever was written. All the balance were shams. Of course the names of the town and territory were a symphony in black, and Tom cannot look upon them to this day without a quiver about the heart. Sitting there in a perfect delirium of bliss, what did he care for the death struggle of nations across the seas? Did the question of "tariff" bother him, then? No; he even forgot the "negro problem" of his own loved South. He was foolishly happy without knowing or inquiring why.

When he had studied the address for a length of time that denoted a sad lack of learning, or unaccountable absent-mindedness, he kissed the letter and felt in his pocket for his knife. He would not tear a

thing so precious, lest a portion of it be lost or disfigured, so opening the smallest blade of the knife he
carefully cut one end of the envelope, and his heart
was almost still as he drew forth a dainty, perfumed
paper. There came again the old-time Sunday morning odor of violets as he opened the letter and looked
with trembling to its contents. Did it commence
"Dear Tom," or any of the old familiar terms of long
ago? Ah, no! What he read was this:

"Miss Madge Carter's compliments to Mr. Thomas
Mabry "——

Then she invited him to be present at the closing
concert of her school on the last evening of July.
That was all. There was no pretty little postscript,
such as loving woman always adds to her letter;
nothing upon which to hang a hope, and the day
became suddenly dark, nor did the valley seem quite
so fair. The lines grew hard about Tom's mouth, and
the buoyancy of a few minutes ago was all gone. It
was as when a northeast storm suddenly obscures a
spring day, and the birds cease singing while the sun
is in hiding. You think your fate is cruel, Tom, but
the day is coming when this little touch of winter
will be forgotten amid the wild desolation of a tempest that shall overwhelm you. But the storm will pass.

The first shock of disappointment over, there came
a revulsion of feeling. The intense love was hidden,
not drowned, by the angry tide that swept up in his
heart, and Tom in his anger became unjust.

"She is cruel and heartless! Her compliments, indeed—when I would give my right arm for one kind word, and sell my soul for her smile. Compliments! I won't have them. She has no doubt sent such stuff as that to a dozen of the boys in Feliciana, and they are crowing over it like a parcel of bantams."

Then stuffing the letter into his pocket the wrathful young man plunged down the hill and into the house with a bang, not stopping to kiss his mother or Janet, but rushed into his room, and, drawing out his desk, settled himself to write.

"Gracious!" exclaimed his sister. "What ails our Tom this evening? He's in a terrible tantrum."

"Something has troubled the dear boy, and I must see what it is," replied her mother, and going to his door the good woman knocked and entered into the presence of her son.

"Why, Tom, my dear boy, something has happened to distress you. Are you well?"

"Yes, mother, I am well, but something has happened to distress me. Read that, will you?" and he handed her the invitation, all the while writing away like his life depended upon it.

"I do not see anything to trouble one about this," said his mother. "It is a very pretty and polite invitation from Madge for you to attend the closing concert of her school. You ought to go if you can, and I have no doubt you and she will settle your little differences. You are a pair of foolish children anyhow— loving each other and yet too proud to yield a point.

You'd feel precious badly cut up if she had forgotten to invite you."

"Well, mother, I've answered that important missive, and you may read what I've said. Here it is."

The dear woman read Tom's answer and hardly knew whether to laugh or cry, but upon a moment's reflection she laughed. This is what the wrathful young man had written:

"Mr. Thomas Mabry's compliments to Miss Madge Carter, and he begs to assure her that it will be utterly impossible for him to attend the concert spoken of in her kind invitation. He feels sure that he will not be missed from the throng who will crowd to admire the fair graduate."

"You don't know how heartless that will seem to your little sweetheart, my dear boy, and if you will wait until morning you will not send it," continued his mother; but Tom was sulky, and her prophecy was only partially true.

Soothed by a cup of Mrs. Mabry's excellent tea, and satisfied with a plateful of her famous biscuit, the young man was no longer hungry, and by bed-time he was at peace with all the world. The next morning when the first rays of sunshine came streaming into the valley from beyond the hills of Quimby, our Tom plunged with a whoop into the trout-stream and paused amid the glories of an ante-breakfast bath to note the mocking echoes of every hillside. A night of perfect rest, a plunge in delicious waters, and a good breakfast, will calm the angriest of angry passions; hence our hero was ready to forgive his little Princess, and bless her for recollecting him at all. He added a postscript to his letter of the night before, and this was what he said:

"Madge, dear, when I wrote the above I was a brute, but now I am your own loving Tom, as of old. Last night I dreamed that you were the same delightful little Madge who played the game of mumble-the-peg with me so long ago under that dear old beech tree which you and I can never forget. Your note was such a disappointment to me, although I have kissed it a hundred times. If you would really be glad to see me, Madge, darling—and I am sure of it—answer this and I will come to you. Oh, Madge! Madge! I would give the world if we could be to each other as of old. Waiting for your answer and yearing to see you once again, I shall try to be patient until it comes."

Then posting it he went about his duties with a hopeful heart. Speed, little letter! Be you never so careful, mail carrier! for loving hearts are waiting to break should you fail in your duty.

Out at his post working like a hero all those July days, and dreaming as he carved the mighty hills, Tom saw but few of the morning papers, and if he read the account of a train wreck at Vattel's creek, in Ohio, he did not know that his fateful letter was burned with the mail, and that on the concert night amid the Virginia hills sweet Madge's voice quivered as she sang her farewell song, for looking over the vast audience she missed the one familiar face that was dearer to her than all the world besides.

Weeks grew into months, and the poor fellow haunted the post-office until the unsentimental person in charge noted the disappointed look and spoke a tender negative to the vain inquiry for a letter. This fond hope died away, and as the burden of his great sorrow became heavier than he could bear he cast it upon Him who promised to the finally faithful a crown in exchange for the cross. Then his heart grew lighter, and abundant peace made the world seem fair once more. If possible he was tenderer with mother and Janet; then came a day when the sweet sister placed her fair hand in that of the gallant Chief Engineer and went away to a city home.

Did Madge doubt the faith of her boy lover? Not without assistance, and many years passed ere Tom learned that one whom he trusted and loved had poisoned her mind, although her gentle heart could never be turned away from him. Had she gotten the lost letter perhaps this story would never be written; but the letter never reached its destination, and not until the angels roll the stone away shall we know what "might have been."

Another winter threw its icy fetters about the western mountains, to be broken only when the winds came up from the South and called the violets from out the snow. The tender beauty of another spring time gladdened **every heart,** and then the summer came to clothe the hills with green and azure.

One year has passed since Tom wrote his last letter to Madge. We see him stronger, sterner and manlier than of yore, yet with the same kindly word for his friends, and a stronger purpose to win his way to fame and fortune. His mail is a large budget now, for he is a man of much business; but nothing was ever read with the interest bestowed upon the little missive of one year ago. It was filed away with the deed to his farm. Tom had a heavy mail this afternoon, and as he walked home he stopped again to rest upon the table-rock and overlook his letters. There was one from the president of the road commending him for a masterly piece of tunneling; and one from a poor widow, whose son had broken a limb while working for the company, thanking him for twenty dollars he had sent her in time of distress. There were letters of inquiry and letters of complaint, all of which were duly considered; and then as he sat in the cool shade he turned listlessly to his newspapers. He glanced at the telegrams, mining news and railway notes, then opening a forlorn-looking little package he beheld a copy of the old familiar paper published in his boyhood home. Some officious friend had sent it. Glancing with some interest at the column of local news he suddenly turns faint, and as the blood leaves his face he clasps his hands upon his breast to stop the spasm of pain that pressed about his heart.

Was some dear one dead and this the funeral message? Yes, the little Princess of his boyhood, and the star of his young manhood, was dead; forever dead to him!

This was what he read:

"MARRIED, at the residence of the bride's father, on Thursday morning, July 2d, Miss Madge Carter to John Boswell, Esq., of New Orleans. The happy couple left on the 10 o'clock train for New York, where they will embark for Europe and remain until the end of the year."

The sinking sun ere it passed behind the western hills peeped under the trees and saw a man lying like one dead upon the smooth surface of the table-rock. Two hours later, when the tender stars looked down in pity, they shone upon the haggard face of that man staggering along down the path; and the angels heard his cry as he fell into the mother's faithful arms:

"Oh, mother! I am most miserable!"

* * * * * *

Madge was out upon the ocean ere Tom came back to life and loved ones out of the deep spell into which he had fallen, and when he went back to his post with a tinge of frost about his once dark hair, she was wandering amid the crumbling glories of Rome, and trying in vain to forget the boy lover who had gone away into the West and out of her life. Why she married we cannot tell. The whims of a woman are past finding out, but her heart is always right. Here is one of

those partings so common in real life, and, except in
dreams, here must Tom and Madge bid each other an
eternal farewell.

It is very common in writing for the novelist to
bring together again those loving souls so sadly parted,
but this is not a novel. All the way it has been a
history of those who lived and loved. The solemn
impress of truth is upon every page. The world is
better because some of the characters of this story lived.
It would be easy to kill off John Boswell, but we shall
let him live and take his chances. We have further
use for Tom, for he has just now begun to live, and we
think we see where the cloud will lift from his soul.
The poor fellow shall have a living chance for happiness after all his sorrows. He is a soul that can suffer
and be strong. If he felt the pang of disappointment
in his soul, he bent to his work for solace and sought
forgetfulness amid his books. One day he came across
a tiny volume, the gift of a dear, dead friend, and read
there a pencilled passage which struck his fancy: ·

> " The years will bring new faces,
>   And as the summer rain
> Falls soft on withered places
>   And makes them green again,
> So time will soften sorrow
>   And lives now overcast
> Shall in some happier morrow
>   Find solace for the past."

"Yes," he exclaimed, "the poet is right, and he
mixes sense with sentiment. I must be a man now,
and since Madge is dead to me I will with an earnest

life build a monument over the grave of my lost love. May you be happy, my lost little Princess, and may you never know how great is the burden of sorrow you placed upon your old-time lover. Life is too short for idle regrets, and I shall look for the ' happier morrow ' amid new duties and new faces."

Under the skillful hand of the young engineer the mighty heart of the Rockies was pierced, and another great artery of commerce pulsated under the power of steam. Sometimes in a quiet hour Tom would think what his life might have been, but he would summon his will power and fling away those dreams, and then go about his duties with gentle words for his employees and careful regard for every detail of his work. He was kind to his men, and listened patiently to their complaints. His tender solicitude about the condition of those who were from time to time injured in the work of construction won for him the love of the rough fellows all about him, and the day was rapidly approaching when that love would form a living wall between him and destruction—when their cheerful shouts would nerve his arm to new endeavors and renew hope in his despairing heart.

Tom always held to the principle that those hardworking men were not of another clay, but were brothers, quickly amenable to the law of kindness. If there was trouble about the wages he always took up for his men, and during the great financial troubles of 1873, when railroad building was paralyzed all over the country, they clung to him with a fidelity that

11

astonished the officers of this great corporation and
stimulated them to unlock their private coffers to feed
the faithful fellows. Thus passed two years of labor
and progress, until in the summer of 1875 Colonel
Elmore was elected vice-president of the road, and our
young man stepped up into a position the duties of
which had been measurably upon his shoulders for a
long while,

One day soon after this, Tom was in that marvelous
marvel, called Leadville, and as he reached the point
where Six-shooter Avenue intersects Whiskey Straight,
he heard a noise of shouting and wild laughing. It was
very much such a hurrah as arouses the average village when an unfortunate dog moves out into the sub-
urbs with a tin can addition to its tail. A great crowd
of loafers and gamblers were yelling and tossing their
hats in the air, while all interest seemed to be centered
upon some object which our young engineer could not
see. Suddenly from out the crowd there rushed in
frantic haste a fat little man, bareheaded and scared.
His coat was a fashionable wreck, being torn from the
tail nearly to the neck, and each division of the tail
was standing out on its own responsibility as he ran,
or rather waddled up the street. The poor fellow was
running his best in an aimless sort of a way, and after
him, like grim death, came a red-faced ruffian who occasionally fired a shot over the head of the fugitive to
stir him up to greater speed, yet all the time yelling
for the poor wretch to stop. As the miserable man
reached the crossing Tom recognized him, and calling

him to come over to his side of the street, assured him
of protection. Surprise almost conquered fear as the
man caught sight of our Tom, and shouting at the top
of his voice—

"Help, Tom Mabry, help! That devil will kill me!"
he started across the avenue, but his sorrows were not
yet at an end. His pursuer was now very close and the
sharp report of another pistol shot only stirred him up
for greater speed, when an unlucky rock spun away
from under his foot, rolling him into the dirt, where he
surrendered.

Tom sprang quickly to his assistance, and was about
to raise the unfortunate man, when the harsh voice of
the ruffian called out:

"None of that, now! Let him alone—he's my meat!"
but paying no heed to this warning, he stooped to
help the fallen man to his feet. As he looked up a
pistol, propelled by a monstrous oath, was thrust against
his face, splitting the skin upon the cheek and nearly
hurling him to the earth. Quick as thought he pushed
the weapon aside, and springing up planted a powerful
blow square in the fellow's face. It was a good blow,
well delivered, and under it the ruffian went down.
Before he could recover Tom was upon him and had
him disarmed, but the ruffian had friends near, who
rushed to the rescue, and to face a crowd of angry men
with an empty pistol is a very delicate matter. He
stood holding them at bay with the presented weapon,
but things looked squally for our hero. With terrible
oaths the angry mob rushed upon him, but gave back

as more than one felt the weight of a pistol barrel upon
his head. Tom was wondering how it would all end,
and was wishing himself well back in his car, when a
man sprang out from the crowd of spectators now gathered around and a cheerful voice called—

"Stand up to them, **Mr.** Mabry! Back, you cowardly devils, and let's have fair play! Boys, it's our
old boss, Tom Mabry, and nobody shall hurt him
while I'm here!"

Instantly a great shout went up from the crowd on
the sidewalk, and a dozen stout fellows rushed to the
rescue, with such a show of determination that the
gamblers felt their courage ebb away. Those men who
came so timely were of the little army who had worked
under Tom's orders and experienced his kindness on
all occasions.

"I am more than proud to see you, boys," said Tom,
"and I thank you for saving my life from that mob.
You all know me, and should any one of you ever
need help you always know where to find your old-
time boss. I want you all to come around to Bucka-
lew's to-day and you shall eat with me the best dinner
this town affords."

"Hurrah for Tom Mabry!" shouted the happy fellows, and the crowd echoed the sentiment until for a
few minutes our young engineer was the most popular
man in Leadville. Then turning to the poor trembling
fellow who was seated on a box, the living image of
misery and discomfort, he reached out his hand and

said: "Come, get up, John Barton, and tell me why you are here, and what all this trouble is about."

They walked away to John's lodgings, where, after he had exchanged his torn coat and made himself presentable, they sat down and he told his version of the affair. John Barton had never married, but upon the remnant of his wealth had contrived to live so well that during the ten years since we saw him a dapper young officer at Richmond, he had added vastly to his flesh and parted with the most of his hair.

"Well you see, Tom," he said, "these damned fellows don't know a gentleman when they meet one. I had gone into a saloon to get me a cocktail when I found a great crowd of motley fellows hurrahing about the bar, and I would have retreated, but as I attempted to back out they stopped me and swore I had to drink with them. They were celebrating the good luck of a miner who had just 'struck it rich' in the mines, as they say. I told them that I generally selected my company when I took a drink, and this seemed to make them mad. Then they took hold of me and tried to make me drink, which of course I resisted. In the struggle they knocked off my hat, tore my coat most shamefully, and, by heavens, sir! they were about to drench me as you would a colicky horse, when I tore away from them and ran out the door. That red-faced devil—may old Nick burn him a thousand years!—drew his six-shooter and commenced firing at me, and if I had'nt run upon a friend there's no telling what would have happened.

I expect I should have been compelled to stop and take the life of the scoundrel. Oh, this is a sweet-scented town! A gentleman feels as lonesome here as a fiddler would in heaven!"

Tom could not help from smiling at this recital, but was too polite to laugh, as his feelings suggested, and he commiserated with the unfortunate fellow in the best style he could command. He insisted that in this rough country it was always best to humor the whims of the wild fellows who infest it, when you can do so consistently. They often meant no harm, but hen they got hold of a "tenderfoot" they generally had some fun.

"I came up here," resumed Barton, "to invest in mining property, but I think this kind of life will not suit me. Free niggers and cotton have nearly bank-rupted me, but I would rather endure all the vexations of farm life in Louisiana than accumulate wealth in this ante-chamber of hell. A man is not safe here a minute, for if he don't get a bullet that is aimed at him he will pick up one intended for another person. I am not yearning for that kind of death. I used to be a desperate fellow in the old days when there was some credit in getting shot, but I am wiser now. I have found out that for all the fuss they make people have very little use for a dead man. It would be awfully inconvenient to die just now."

"I think," replied Tom, "that you would not find this life suited to one of your temperament, and I would advise you to return at once to Louisiana. We must

adapt ourselves to the people and circumstances surrounding us if we would succeed."

A few hours later Tom bade his old-time enemy
good-bye at the depot, and as the St. Louis express
thundered away it carried John Barton out of sight and
away from our story.

The hairs of his head are easy to number now, and
a pair of scales is his abhorrence.

CHAPTER XX.

MANY of our readers doubtless think it is high time for us to dispose of Tom. The poor fellow has met many disappointments thus far in life, but the fires have only refined the pure gold of his nature. It takes some sorrows and disasters to round out the character of a young man. They strengthen and develop his soul as healthful exercise hardens the muscles. Yes, it is time to dispose of Tom. We have not shielded him, but have exposed his foibles until the world can judge how well he deserved his troubles. Prosperity has followed his earnest labors and he has the unlimited confidence of his great corporation. We have something good in store for him yet, and then we shall part. We have endeavored to record faithfully the lives of two boys, well remembered in Feliciana. Our task is nearly done. Could we have saved the gallant Joe, ah! how lovingly would we cling to him until the trembling pen refused to move. It is very difficult for us to become reconciled to some of the tragedies of real life, and no lapse of time can quiet the rebellious heart. Tom has arrived at that mature age and condition when he no longer takes pleasure in "dream life," but peruses the financial

(248)

columns of the morning papers, and discusses the tariff or other political problems. He is a man of business now. He wears shoes with broad soles and flat heels, while his feet revel in all the "elbow-room" necessary for comfort. His tastes have changed. It is doubtful if Aunt Viney's potato pone would attract him as of old, and a game of mumble-the-peg would not arouse more than a passing emotion. We are not so sure about the marbles. The swimming hole at fair Belhaven is only suggestive of muddy feet and musquitoes. He would laugh at the idea of cavalry boots and variegated neckties. The trouble with Tom is that his boyhood is forever gone.

Most of the actors in this story have passed away from us during these fifteen years, and so it will ever be as long as people live, and love, and die. We know where dear Joe and the young Georgian sleep under the moaning pine, and memory—oh, so tender! will ever cling about that lonely grave; our hearts yearned over sweet Jennie as the grief-stricken little woman vanished in the twilight; we heard the volley over the grave of the disappointed and repentant Pete Brownlow; everybody rejoiced over the good fortune and happiness of the giant North Carolinian, and saw the sunset flush when the noble old judge entered into rest. Goodnight has cared for "poor little fool Si Owens," and John Barton has bidden the wild west an eternal farewell. Colonel DuPree has grown fat, and still talks "State rights" between naps as he sits on his piazza during the long summer afternoon, while Major Carter, still proud and stately, rejoices in the good things of life, and occasionally occupies his pew in the old hill-country church. The brave and handsome Captain Ransome hung his saber upon the wall and has gone to Congress from Mississippi. He is a "Colonel" now. Is there any one left? If not, we must dispose of the lonely Tom. It would be cruel to leave him desolate. Despite the fact that he is a business man, he often sits in the gathering twilight, and as his soul looks back across the distant years—dreams.

But stop! Did we not in the early days of our story catch a glimpse of a pretty little maiden with brown ringlets, who clapped her chubby hands when the mighty steamer bore our hero and his fortunes down the great Father of Waters? Certainly we did. She was a very wee maiden away back yonder in 1853, but she has had ample time to grow during twenty years, and no doubt the pretty curls have changed into a classic twist upon a stately head—so there are yet two characters to be disposed of, else the record might close just here.

Tom was well to do now. He had taken care of his excellent salary paid him during the past five years and had made some successful mining ventures. His valley home was perhaps as lovely a spot as could be found in beautiful Colorado, but it lacked a mistress since his mother had gone to live with Janet in her city home. Sometimes he wished for some one to help admire his splendid herd of Jerseys. His gun and dog were boon companions often, but even these wearied him. and his guitar stood in one corner with a broken string. There was nothing homelike in the hotel where he took his meals, and the accumulation of partly-worn garments in his wardrobe was becoming a burden. A woman in the household would have settled all those troubles, and many a poor tramp would have gone away clothed and impudent. In short, Tom was now twenty-six years of age and began to realize that it was not good, nor pleasant, for man to be too much alone. The little god was about to make a target of our hero once more, and was already whetting his arrows for the conflict.

The pretty town of Quimby had been growing, and the tourist from the East or the far South often stopped there to enjoy the delightful summers. In the spring of 1876 Tom resigned his position with the railroad to accept the office of president in a new national bank just organized to meet the wants of the growing town, and there he found a field for the display of all his executive ability. Had he been in a large city perhaps he would have expanded to meet the greater requirements of such a place, but he had been raised a country lad and his ideas were scarcely metropolitan.

As he went home from the bank one afternoon in August there were two ladies sitting upon the famous table-rock. One of these ladies was a fine looking, matronly woman of fifty, and the other, who seemed to be her daughter, was very fair, with just such a suspicion of roses in her cheek as indicated good health. Tom lifted his hat as he passed, and so far forgot his good manners as to look back a time or two ere he

reached the valley.   That night he mended the broken
string of his guitar, and may be he sang an old love
song, but only Queen Dido, the pointer, and his mild-
eyed Jerseys heard the music.   When he went to sleep
he dreamed such dreams as only visit the pillow of a
pure-hearted, vigorous young man

A few days later the two ladies visited the bank
upon some monetary matter—for even the women,
dear creatures, are compelled to have money in this
sordid world—and from the little item of business it
was very easy for Tom to lead them into a spritely
conversation, which lasted perhaps twenty minutes.
The bank clerks wondered what made their superior
so loath to let the ladies depart, and when they did
leave the teller whispered to the book-keeper—

"That's a dog-gone pretty girl!"

Of course the young man meant no disrespect by
this irreverent remark, but all boys who do not actually
swear roll this expressive word under their tongues as
a sweet morsel and fire it off on the slightest provocation.   We doubt if there is a boy in America who has
not at some time or other used this expression in some
of its moods, or tenses, and felt relieved.   It is a sort
of compromise when we are angry and our aroused
consciences cry out against profanity; but oftener it
it merely comes as an idle word which we are told will
be reckoned for on some dismal day in the hereafter.

Ere long the gossips of Quimby declared that the
young bank president was smitten with the fair tourist, Miss Edith Gordon, and that the young lady was

very gracious. Certain it is that the best carriage of
the one livery stable in the village was occupied every
bright afternoon by a gentleman and two ladies, who
seemed to be wonderfully fond of the mountain scenery,
and hardly a day passed but the general health of the
party required that they should drink of a certain
mineral spring a few miles down the valley. It is also
certain that on Sunday the two young people used the
same song book at church—books being scarce in
frontier churches—and as Edith's rich soprano filled
all the air with melody, Tom almost forgot his bass
while listening. The faithful preacher, whose salary
was an unknown quantity, could almost hear the music
of wedding bells as he looked upon the charming
couple.

Tom showed the ladies his pretty home, and listened
with complacency to their raptures over his herd of
poetic Jerseys, or envied Queen Dido certain demonstrations of fondness at the hands of the young lady.
Then, one day when the tourists started back to their
Louisiana home, he found that business required a trip
to St. Louis in the same train that carried the ladies.
The truth of the whole matter is that our Tom had
calmly, deliberately, and "with sedate mind," as the
lawyers say, fallen again into his most prominent
youthful habit—and into love.

Love is a fever, not like measles or yellow fever of
which there is no return, but dangerous, inasmuch as
no man ever gets too old to be attacked. The fever may
cool and the patient be pronounced entirely well, when

some unfortunate exposure, or lawn party, will bring on another attack until the poor fellow becomes real silly.

When Tom bade Edith good-bye at the steamer, he suddenly felt a great yearning for his old Southland home, and declared that he would spend his next Christmas in Louisiana. He begged that he might visit the fair girl at her home, and then he returned to Quimby to find that never within the memory of the oldest and most truthful inhabitant, had the autumn months taken so long to pass by. Every day seemed about twenty-four hours long, and, but for the fact that he had an easy conscience, with good digestion, the nights would have tallied another score. But the weeks and months will hurry by, sometimes with a speed that makes us dizzy, and when, at the close of another year, we try to reckon its profits and losses, the balance sheet appalls us.

Again the winter came thundering down from far off icy regions, spreading over mountain, plain and valley, as the Goths and Vandals desolated the fair campania about the Roman city. Beneath its cold touch, flower and herb grew brown and rigid; the trout brook hushed its pretty lullaby; the towering hills grew white, and the song of birds was heard no more. Tom stood upon the table-rock listening to the migration notes of the wild goose, and he remembered that in two days more it would *honk* with joy amid the rice and cane fields of his own Louisiana.

Did no ghost of the past haunt this pleasant faced young man, as he looked with impatience to his Southern visit? Was the memory of the long-ago scene beneath the old beech-tree at Belhaven dead? Who talks of undying love in this world of broken vows? If love lives forever; if the divine essence must exist in spite of forgotten vows and broken hearts, it teaches a doctrine of transmigration as it speeds from the wreck of to-day, and fills to-morrow with sunshine.

Ah, no! the memory of that other love was not dead with Tom, but put away under some secret lock, and the key cast into the fathomless depths of "Nevermore." That night a faded note, taken from alongside the deed to the home, was wrapped about a sweet girl's photograph, and both disappeared forever from mortal vision. There was a shade of sorrow about the blue eyes as the flames obscured their beauty, but the sunny smile rose up with the curling smoke and filled the room as burning incense filled the holy place.

At the next meeting of the bank directory, Tom left that institution in their charge, and sped away to look after certain interests away down in the low country, where the Mississippi rushes to the sea.

Two days before Christmas, the steamer Great Republic on its way to New Orleans, rounded to in the early morning at a plantation landing not many miles below Vicksburg, and as the giant vessel turned at the pilots touch, her brazen mouth-piece boomed out a note of warning that startled every sleeping echo for twenty miles around, and awoke many an ancient darkey from happy dreams of "possum and taters." There was some little commotion at the house and

quarters, for whilst coast packets were an every day
occurrence, it was not often that they saw a grand up-
country steamer, except as it swept proudly past on its
way to the Crescent City. As usual, quite a lot of
negroes turned out to see the steamer land. Some
came to make themselves useful, but the majority because they had no business there.

"Name o' Gawd!" exclaimed old Uncle Tom, the
good-natured major-domo of the carriage-house. "Jess
lissen at de Graterpublic beller! Holler like he own.
dis whole plantashun an' dun cum fer it. I'm gwineter run over to de lebby an' pick up a quarter from sum
white man fo' sum dem new-issue niggers gets in erhead
o' me."

Then the old man dropped the brush with which he had
been tickling Lightfoot and hurried away to the landing

"What de debbil dat big boat mean trineter cave off
a aker o' dis farm at one time?" queried young Bullet,
as he sauntered leisurely down to the landing with the
regulation "one gallus," and his old slouched hat stuck
rakishly over his left ear. "Gwineter buss dis lebby
plum open wid her *ting-a-ling-ling, tong-a-long-long,
tchow! tchow!* an' dem niggers hollerin wid dat gang-
plank like sumbody drap hot ashes in da shoes. Bet
a hundred dollers da got ter pay fer dat aker o' lan,
else ole Miss Gord'n gwineter takum to der cote house
sho! Run out dat line dare, you blac rascals, fo' I buss
you open wid dis stick o' cawd wood!" This last
remark was directed to the roustabouts of the boat—at
a safe distance.

While the old negro still clings to his ancient habit of calling upon the name of deity on every trivial occasion, the young "new-issue-nigger" is equally certain to invoke the devil. The old slave means no harm, and in his simple ignorance clings to his long-formed habits, but the young freedman appeals to his patron in utter wantonness. He would not mend his ways under anything short of a Ku-klux visitation.

All this hurrah in the early morning resulted in landing one passenger, and our Tom giving his old namesake the expected quarter with his valise to carry, walked to the house with a degree of apparent unconcern that won for him the respect of every darkey who beheld him.

"Man, ser!" exclaimed Aunt Eunice, the cook, who from her kitchen window could command the walk to the landing. "He holes heself up like a shorenuf white man. I 'low he's dat young bankerman what I hyeard Marse Bob a teasin' Miss Edy about. I do think on my soul Marse Bob is de devilishest white man I ever seed in all my born days! He is that agryvatin, an' there ain't no time but what he's a teasin' an' a worryin' Miss Edy or Ole Miss. I lay Miss Edy 'll hafter marry dat man jess so she can go way an' git shet o' dat onregenerate brother o' hern. But, law! Marse Bob don't mean no meanness in his debblement, fer he's jest as good to his sister as he kin be—'ceppen his mischief. Ef dat white man is de right kind o' 'stockracy he kin marry Miss Edy, if she'll let him, an' ef he ain't he kaint."

Tom was very kindly received and spent one blissful week on the plantation. Buggy rides along the
smooth river road and under the leafless branches of
the great trees; never to be forgotten strolls along the
levee, listening to the murmur of the great river and
to the music of their own voices; songs and games by
lamplight in the parlor; stately dinners where Uncle
Tom officiated in the blackest of coats and whitest
of aprons; cosy teas that make a man forget he ever
had a trouble or a sorrow; sweet whispered confidences
in the moonlight that was filling all the Southland with
splendor, and a formal conference or "family meeting"
to name the day—for Tom and Edith had wandered
into each other's hearts and avowed their mutual happiness—all rounded out the seven days' visit, and made
our quondam engineer feel that life was worth living
a thousand years. He wanted to know why the wedding could not take place at once, but when he noted
the look of polite surprise upon the face of his intended
mother-in-law he offered no more propositions, but let
that worthy lady arrange matters to suit herself, while
he discussed with the sedate Bob the relative merits
of the "levee" and the "outlet" systems for the great
river.

Three weeks was the shortest time possible to arrange
for the marriage, and even that was considered a con-
cession to the calls of business which ought not to be
established as a precedent, then Tom went away down
the river to visit other friends, and relapsed into his
old time habit of dreaming.

How long and how short is the time comprised in
the measure of three weeks! The queen who offered
millions of money for minutes of time, would have
bankrupted the nation in three weeks, and the man
who waits for the hangman bewails the speed with
which they slip away. But to the anxious lover waiting for the hour that shall link his destiny with the
future of one, who, putting her little hand in his, shall
say: "Thy people shall be my people, and thy God,
my God"—those weeks are all too slow, and even the
hours devoted to dreaming shall loiter by the way.
Yet the time will pass, and we have known a faithful
lover grow old with waiting.

Ah, Tom! your happiness has been long coming,
but the heavens bend down to kiss you now, and the
future seems fairer than a summer day. The storms
are all past, the earthquake throes have ceased, and
there is a feeling of warmth about the heart that proves
the doctrine of love's metempsychosis

    *   *   *   *   *   *   *

Again a mighty steamer is rushing up the great
river. This time the tall young man has grown manlier, and there are no fogs drifting around the vessel.
The lordly sun has gone done into the west, but ere he
sank the earth was crimson with glory and the clouds
were aflame. Then as the purple shadows came streaming across the water and a willow-crowned point shut
away from view her distant home, a fair girl looked up
into Tom Mabry's face and sweet lips murmured ·

"Dear love, I will go with thee, never doubting, even
to the end of the earth."

www.ingramcontent.com/pod-product-compliance
Lightning Source LLC
Chambersburg PA
CBHW031346020726
47499CB00005B/1416